I0573311

THUNDER EDGE

A Novel

By

Sandra Leigh Gable

Launch Point Press
Portland, Oregon
www.LaunchPointPress.com

I dedicate my first story to my faithful and loving sister, Susan R. Kacher-Gremmert, who has always helped get me through tough times.

"There are more things in Heaven
and Earth, Horatio, than are
dreamt of in your philosophy."

Hamlet, Act I, Scene 5

1
Friday the Thirteenth, 1950
Nyah

In a blinding blizzard, I prayed to the gods I wouldn't freeze to death.

I'd spent the daylight hours peddling my artwork door to door to uncaring souls, people going about their own lives hoping to survive the dreaded winter storm. Bone-tired, about to drop, I shifted my portfolio from under one arm to the other. My fingers and toes were frozen. Heavy slanting snow blasted my face—tears froze on my cheeks. The deafening storm howled around me and into my ears through my earmuffs. I bundled my tattered gray scarf tighter around my neck and glanced at my mismatched gloves. The brown one was much better at keeping out the cold than the thinner green one.

The Puget Sound park, in the middle of the uptown neighborhood, was vacant, as most residents were home with their families and pets bundling together in front of their wood-burning fireplaces trying to stay warm. The long row of park benches stretching to Tibbals Lake had three feet of snow piled on them, and the light posts were so heavily laden that any illumination shone dimly.

Snow melted into my eyes blurring my vision. Unable to lean forward far enough to get my legs under me, I fell hard, slipping and falling again and again into the collapsing drifts. A surge of panic racing through me, I released my portfolio hoping to save myself from being buried.

My breathing was shallow. My blood banged against both sides of my neck. I staggered to my feet, leaned against a light post, and puked acrid green and yellow bile into the snow. My heart pounded.

The edge of my portfolio jutted out of the snow. I wrenched it loose, falling on my knees. My surroundings whirled around me. I managed to stand, but my muscles cramped and pulled me back down onto my knees.

I rose and teetered forward with my portfolio under my arm—frozen, unblinking, staring into the snowbank. I stepped forward, stopped, stepped forward again. My brain was inexplicably empty. *Where am I? Who am I?* After a few steps, I recalled my name: *Nyah, Nyah James. I live in Port Townsend on the Quimper Peninsula in Washington state and I'm an artist trying to find my way home.*

The only sounds were the muted crunch of my footfalls on the crust of the hard-packed snow. The air smelled like the inside of my refrigerator. I approached the steep hill. A howl of wind knocked me sideways. A surge of ice snaked up my spine. Immediately, the once dimly lit park glimmered bright yellow through the muffled evening mist with a delicate dusting of ice-blue snow on the leaf-bare branches and the park benches. The temperature rose measurably.

My ears popped.

I felt a tingling sensation as though time had altered my reality; a quiver unfurled from the back of my neck to my shoulder blades. My first thought: hallucinations had invaded my muddled brain due to starvation and my baffled state of mind. I heard a whisper, a song of sorts, faint, but distinct.

A shadow resembling a child perched in the middle of one of the park benches. I leaned against a tree trunk and squinted. The shape of the tiny body transformed into the silhouette of a wee girl holding a red-cheeked ragdoll in her lap. The closer I stepped toward her the more luminous was the child's face. The doll had bright red yarn hair, a triangular red nose, and long red and white stockings. Gathering my equilibrium, I staggered toward the child. She stopped singing and looked up at me smiling. A lilac-colored luminosity wrapped around her.

"Are you okay, honey?" I asked. "Are you lost?"

The little girl looked to be age five, possibly six. She wore no coat or jacket or hat or gloves. And against nature, the girl didn't shiver.

"The nice lady wants to know if we're lost," she said to the doll.

I waited for the child to answer my questions, but she pressed her lips together and only looked at me

"What a pretty dress," I said. The child wore a clean, sleeveless dress sewn out of white flour sacks with red crocheted rosebuds stitched into the fabric. Affixed around the high collar were yellow and black life-size honeybees which appeared to be handsewn, the threads frayed. The tiny cherub's arms and legs were reedy twigs, and her shoes were stitched together in layers of flour sacks. No human would allow a child to be out in the snow without a coat, hat, and rubber boots. I wondered about her parents' means of support. I knew how it felt to be alone, cold, and poor.

"Mommy made my dress from flour sacks. Mommy made my sister, Annie, a dress like mine. Mommy did the best she could."

"Your mommy? She must be frantic wondering where you are."

The little phantom squeezed her cherry red lips together and said nothing.

"Which house do you live in? I'll get you home safely." I stepped closer to her. "What's your name?"

The little girl glanced into the face of her ragdoll. "My name is Lulu."

"Lulu? What's your last name, Lulu?"

She didn't answer. I reached out my hand hoping she would trust me.

Gripping the ragdoll, the child clambered down from the bench. "We would like to walk with you." She lifted her chin high enough to gaze into my eyes.

Hastily, I unwrapped my neck scarf and unbuttoned my jacket. "Don't be afraid, Lulu. I'm going to wrap this jacket around you, okay?"

"Okay."

Little Lulu was no taller than my hipbone. I was five-foot-two. Her hair color matched her ragdoll's curls, but unlike the black button eyes of her doll, the tiny girl's eyes were turquoise, framed within blond eyelashes with a sparkle of pink tint at the end of each lash. Her scent was lavender buds.

"I'm not cold."

"May I wrap my jacket around you while we stroll together?"

"Why yes, it'll be okay; but I'm warm enough."

I draped my jacket over her shoulders anyway, pulled up the collar around the back of her head, and tied my threadbare scarf around her tiny waist. Without a thought, I put my wool earmuffs on her head and did my best to cover her ears.

"Which way is your house? I'll get you home safely." I quivered from the sudden icy air. "Whatever happened to your coat and hat? Did you drop them somewhere?"

"Now you're cold," she said, ignoring my question.

"No, I'm not cold, honey." As I spoke, I realized the wind had abated, and it wasn't so bitterly cold after all. "Where do you live? It's getting late."

"I live on the other side of the lake. It's not far." She grasped my gloved hand and tugged me gently forward. "Is it late? I never think about time." Her doll's feet trailed lightly along the path in the snow, leaving featherlike imprints.

I shifted my portfolio to the other arm, took off the brown glove and shoved it in my pocket. The child again gripped her warm hand into mine. At first she felt unreal, but the warmth of her skin against mine eased my rising anxiety that she might be a figment of my imagination.

"Me and my sister, we live at the orphanage. Annie has a bad cough. She can't breathe very good. We won't be missed. We take care of each other."

"What happened to your parents?"

The tiny girl didn't answer.

A lilac-colored mist swirled around us like an excited apparition. The hairs on the back of my neck bristled. Despite her calm appearance, my anxious tension gave me a sick sensation, not because I was hungry. I questioned my sanity. Meandering around Tibbals Lake with her tiny hand nestled inside mine gave me the creeps.

As we strolled along the snowy parkway, oddly enough I didn't feel as cold as I thought I would. I looked for another person, or a dog perhaps, that might be searching for the child, but the park was void of anything except for the two of us strolling around the lake.

I told her, "I don't know of an orphanage nearby."

"What are you carrying?" she said, again ignoring my statement.

"My paintings. I was trying to sell my work today, but no one was interested in buying."

"I was certain they were paintings."

"What made you think that?"

"I know things."

"What do you mean you know things?" I asked, but she continued her narrative.

"The nuns at the orphanage teach us how to read and how to add and subtract numbers. But I want to travel and to learn history," she said in her tiny, precise voice. "The nuns say Germany's president, a man named Hindenburg, appointed a man named Hitler as the Chancellor of Germany."

"Hitler's reign in Germany was long ago. He committed suicide five years ago."

"I'm sure you're wrong. The nuns told us Hitler is now the Chancellor of Germany. What's your name? You haven't yet told me."

"How is it the nuns let you go out in the weather without boots or a coat or a jacket or even long stockings and a hat?" I asked, ignoring her question.

"We have no friends at the orphanage, my sister and I. Thank you for being my friend. Do you have friends?"

"No, not really," I smiled down at her. How beautiful she was, and such innocence shone in her turquoise eyes.

"You haven't told me your name."

"Nyah. Nyah James."

"Nyah, Nyah James, the orphanage is over by the bluff." She tugged at my hand to lead me up the snow-packed path from the lake. "I made up a song just for you."

"Will you sing it to me?"

I ebb and flow,
I go and go.
I'll follow you,
Wait for me when I do.
My years are long,
You are where I belong.

The words of the eerie song made the hairs on the back of my neck stand on end again. Why would this peculiar tiny person have written a song for me? I tried to pull my hand from her grasp, but she was reluctant to release me. She pulled me close to the silhouetted shadow of a large, looming building and stopped at the foot of the stairs. A horrible smell wafted around me. My belly tightened. My lungs were suffocating from the odor of mold and rotting decay.

Darkened, ghostlike windows stared into the darkness of the surrounding woods. Two black crows perched on the end of a stone rail. An owl cocked its head, watching me. The winter's cool mist mingled with the stench of mildew. The branches of the weeping willow trees were motionless.

The imp lifted her chin as though scrutinizing my thoughts. "Did you like my song?" Before I could answer, she said, "Goodbye. I have to go now. Will we see each other again, Nyah, Nyah James? I'll make a wish we walk together again very soon."

She faced the orphanage. Her feet were tiny, and the stone steps were wide. She crawled up the stairs on her hands and feet, stood, and shuffled to the front door.

"Lulu, there's no lights on. Just a minute, I'll walk you to your room. Lulu?"

But she didn't turn to face me.

I noticed her ragdoll sitting upright in the snow.

"Lulu, wait. You dropped your doll."

I stooped, grabbed the doll, but when I stood Lulu was gone, vanished into a lilac-colored mist. My jacket, gray scarf, and earmuffs were piled in front of the tall door, but she'd left no footprints on the snowy stone stairs.

A gust of ice wind blew over me. My stomach flipped. I scrambled up the stairs and peered through one of the slim windows on either side of the entry door. The interior was pitch black. I pounded on the door, but the sound echoed into the darkness. My arms twitched and my legs shuddered as a bolt of fear shot through me. Still holding my portfolio and the doll, I grabbed my jacket, scarf, and earmuffs then stumbled and fell down the stairs as if in a drunken stupor.

I arrived at the place in the park where I'd first seen Lulu sitting on the park bench. I tightly held the arm of the ragdoll, its feet dragging lightly across the hills of snow. I was weak and tired; my fingers and toes numb to the bone. Then my ears popped; my ears adjusted to the quiet surroundings once again.

The park lights were again dimly lit under the heavy weight of snow. The park benches stretched in a line toward the lake. They had three feet of snow piled on them. The snow pierced my face. Tears dripped down my frozen cheeks. I bundled my scarf around my jacket collar. A shiver spread from the back of my neck to my shoulder blades. A spasm of panic racing down my spine, I tightened my grip on the doll and the portfolio. I prayed again to the gods I wouldn't freeze to death.

2
The One-Eyed Dog Saloon and Café
Nyah

Located in the rain shadow of the Olympic Mountains, Port Townsend, a one-saloon town, was where I lived. My apartment was one flight above the One-Eyed Dog Saloon and Café. The second floor of the Delmonico building was the aging hotel the owners made into a rooming house for folks who were down on their luck.

My room was a six-hundred-square-foot studio with an eastern view of the Port Townsend Marina. Lumbering past the thick bay windows of the saloon, I wasn't surprised to see the bar filled with cherry-cheeked men laughing heartily, slapping each other hard on the back, and fortifying themselves with the warmth alcohol provides. It was tempting to open the door and step inside, but I was broke. I was always broke.

After staggering up thirty creaky stairs, I twisted the tarnished skeleton key in the lock, listened for the familiar click, and rotated the rusted doorknob. The hinges squealed like an alley cat at midnight. God, I thought, I wish Mary would give me another space heater. Chilled to the bone, I wondered if I would ever be warm again. I flipped on the light switch near the door. The one and only lightbulb, aside from the forty-watt light in the bathroom, cast a dim light over my easel. A spider web drooped from the bulb to the cracked window.

The musty scent of my room all but dropped me to my knees. I had bigger dreams than to live out my life in an ancient, dank room, not to mention living above a bar of howling men.

My room was the least expensive in the building, having only a twin bed and a couple of sheets and blankets, a wardrobe closet, a tub, toilet, sink, one space heater, and a cold plank floor. Thank God there was a washing machine at the end of the hallway. To dry my clothes,

I'd rigged a thin rope wall to the wall in the bathroom and let the few clothes I had dry over the bathtub.

I opened a can of chicken noodle soup, dumped it into my one and only saucepan, and heated it on my portable one-burner hotplate. I tossed the soup can toward a brown paper sack I used for garbage, but missed the sack, and the can rolled under the kitchen sink. What the hell, I didn't care. While my soup warmed, I opened the rattling refrigerator door. I found a slice of Wonder Bread and a morsel of cheese in its dark interior. Neither the bread nor the cheese was too moldy to swallow along with my lukewarm soup.

I shoved away my paint brushes, unfinished work, and clean canvases to make a space on the edge of my rickety wooden table and sat down with one of my two soup spoons in hand. The tepid soup warmed my innards.

In the bathroom, I brushed my teeth with Bucky Beaver toothpaste, and afterward fixed my gaze on the single toothbrush leaning against the rim of the cracked blue Mason jar and thought it lonely leaning there all by itself. I wiped my hands on my jeans and switched off the light.

Next, I lifted my paintings from the portfolio and set them against the wall. I placed little Lulu's ragdoll on the floor between two of my paintings of Port Townsend scenes. All my paintings were of Port Townsend: the Bell Tower, the multi-colored sailboats in the marina, uptown's original Victorian mansions, the areas around the Strait of Juan de Fuca, the oldest church on the Washington peninsula, Fort Worden, and Fort Casey. For a moment I pondered whether I could turn away from paintings of the town and start painting people. I was shivering and I was tired.

I punched up my flat, droopy pillow edge best I could, straightened the yellowed bed sheets, put my pajamas on over long johns, and pulled knee-high wool stockings over my leggings. I looked out the window facing the frozen inland bay. The icy wind howled through the window's wooden molding, a haunted, eerie cry. Under my long johns my skin goose pimpled. I hoped the snow and raw ice wind wouldn't find a larger crack to squeeze through into my room. I flipped off the light switch and floundered my way to my bed. I climbed between the sheets and wrapped up to my neck in the threadbare blankets provided by Mary, the hotel manager. Shivering from the top of my scalp to the tips of my toes, I cuddled into my turquoise Indian blanket, lay on my side in the fetal position, and closed my eyes.

My mind wandered back to the little waif in the park who called herself Lulu. I couldn't make sense of how, once we arrived at the orphanage, she disappeared into the lilac-colored mist as though she'd never existed—like sorcery. I couldn't get my mind off the mystifying, haunting song the little girl sang for me:

> *I ebb and flow,*
> *I go and go.*
> *I'll follow you,*
> *Wait for me when I do.*
> *My years are long,*
> *You are where I belong.*

I fell asleep with little Lulu drifting through my mind.

3
The Season of My Shadow
Nyah

I woke up sprawled on the bone-chilling plank floor next to the twin bed, my blankets wrapped tightly around my legs. Fiercely, I kicked the covers loose, rose to my feet and sat on the edge of the bed. The room was midnight black. I'd been dreaming about something terrible and had flung myself out of bed, though I couldn't remember exactly what I'd tried to flee. My soul was seared by loss and deprivation, and I was unprepared for the overwhelming need that gripped and tore at my heart. I was hungry, keen for more than meager food. I rarely had two coins in my pocket to clang together. But being hungry and cold weren't the worst of my desolation. After months of soul searching, I couldn't figure out why my work wouldn't sell. I felt as if I were being held hostage.

Whether it be the angry green deluge of the swelling sea, the playful black and white orca whales, the shimmering Olympic mountains, or the wooden boats sailing the Strait of Juan de Fuca, nothing I painted meant anything to me. A deep-seated fear crowded my brain during daylight hours and hung around my neck like a noose. Worse than the biting air, the howling snow, not having meat or potatoes on the table—my soul was frozen. After weeks of isolation and desperation I had become aware of the stark indifference of the world to my hunger and emotional aching, to my very survival on this earth. Each day the strength and confidence I needed to climb out of bed diminished. I was disappearing down a starless, spiraling pit.

The wind hissed through a crack in the window molding. Snow crept inside the room through the other crack in the window. The built-in steam heater produced little steam or heat, and the portable electric heater the landlord loaned me wouldn't dry my wool socks. Like the wind hissing through the crack in the window, I wished I could scream through a hole I imagined in the top of my head. I staggered to the portable heater in a fit of rage and kicked it. I picked up it up and threw it with all strength I could muster. It crashed against the wall and busted into two large pieces and a dozen small shards.

4
The Cape Flattery Art Gallery
Nyah

My portfolio again under my arm, I stopped in front of the Cape Flattery Art Gallery south of town. I hadn't dropped in for several months; my confidence didn't lead me to believe my work would be good enough to be displayed in an art gallery. A sign in the window advertised a featured artist, Nanny Tarpee. I'd heard of her, one of the leading Laguna Beach watercolorists. Aside from being an up-and-coming painter, she'd played character roles in movies with the likes of Lloyd Bridges and James Dean. The artist, aside from being well-known, was a woman, which gave me the courage I needed.

As I pushed open the heavy door, a tiny bell rang above my head. While I viewed the artist's paintings and art deco pottery, an elderly man about six feet tall walked over and introduced himself as the gallery manager. I recognized him as the man who bought one of my paintings in Portland, Oregon several years back. When I first met him and his male friend, his hair was the color of autumn, golden with orange highlights. With years of time, his thick hair and bushy eyebrows had brightened to snow. His curly locks were clipped short up the back and neatly combed above his ears. His suit was a double-breasted navy-blue pin-striped jacket wide at his shoulders and fitted snugly around his narrow hips. The pleats on his cuffed, loose-fitting slacks were neatly pressed. A pink, blue and green paisley hanky poked out of his breast pocket, and his perfectly ironed shirt was the color of a robin's egg. His gray and pink tie was secured with a sparkling silver tie clip. He wore his gold watch on his right wrist, indicating he was left-handed, and a gold band was on his left hand, third finger. His light gray and white Wingtip loafers added to his knack for style. He was the definition of pomp and splendor. His name was Gilles—Francis, as I recalled.

"Good evening, Miss," he said. "We're about to close our doors for the evening. However, what may I do for you?" He spoke in a slightly high-pitched tone and his fingertips were steepled in front of his chest, featuring trimmed and polished fingernails.

I saw him look down through his round, black, horn-rimmed glasses at the thick portfolio under my arm. He knew at once I wasn't in his establishment to buy art, but rather to try to talk him into buying a piece of my work. I remembered he had a colleague, Kayte Berns, whose duties included purchasing art. Between them, she had the stronger personality to say no to starving artists. I thought she must have gone home, or surely Gilles would have dismissed himself so she could be the one to tell me they wouldn't buy my art. He was too kind to say no. Then the clip clop of a woman's shoes echoed from the hallway.

An hour-glass silhouette of a woman floated down the hallway; black high-waisted trousers rippled around her legs. Her slacks were buttoned down the sides and wide at the cuffs. Striking shoulder pads were sewn into the black tweed jacket extending an inch or two past the edge of her shoulders. Fluffed out of the pocket of her white crepe blouse was a slate gray, sky blue, and salmon-colored scarf. The lady's shoes were made of some sort of reptile with a wedged sole. I guessed her height was about five foot eight. Her wavy, gray hair with steaks of lemon-yellow, softly brushed up the back of her neck in a loose modern hairdo.

"Well, hello, Miss James," Miss Kayte said, shaking my gloved hand. "It's nice to see you again." She wore her round wire eyeglasses on the tip of her short narrow nose, which highlighted her oval-shaped smoke-colored eyes. Her lipstick was scarlet-red, and her forehead was wide, her jaw-line as wide as her forehead. Her diamond studded earrings blinked, reflecting the light of the room.

"Mister Gilles," she said, "are you buying a piece from Miss James?"

"Miss Kayte," I said, speaking before Gilles could respond, "let me show you some of my work."

Gilles gently coughed. "My dear madam, living in this historic town, landscapes are not new to us. These days we buy almost no landscape paintings."

Casting his eyes downward, he tried not to look into my begging eyes but failed. He could tell I was hungry and desperate. "Well, show me what you have," he squeaked.

He and Miss Kayte led me to a table on the far side of the gallery. I took off my gloves and with stiff fingers untied the frayed twine of my portfolio, exposing the top painting. I had little to no hope they would like any of my work. I sensed that all Gilles wanted to do was lock the doors, go home, and sip from a glass of wine with his male friend, whom I'd met a few years ago. Steve, I think, was his name. But the gallery was warm, and I was light-headed and feeling faint.

"I painted these on the beach of Fort Worden. And these at North Beach, and here are a few of Discovery Bay and the Olympic Mountains."

"Landscapes, sorry Miss," he said, and the ends of his mouth dropped into a nervous frown.

I finally hit bottom. My knees were rubber bands. I grabbed onto the edge of the table. The blood in my veins was ice water. I struggled to keep my eyes open. My stomach growled like an orca whale, heard by both of them. The moment caught my throat like a vise.

"Here's a couple of sketches of the lighthouse on the Strait of Juan de Fuca," I said, almost audibly.

Gilles was wringing his hands and scratching the back of his neck, preparing to tell me he wasn't interested in my paintings, when his face lit up. He grinned and reached into my portfolio, picking up a drawing.

"What's this?" he asked. "Look here, Kayte."

I looked over his shoulder. What had I painted that was so remarkable to cause him to grin and become a bit giddy?

"It's merely a sketch I drew of a little girl I met in the park a few days ago." I must have put it in my portfolio without thinking.

"This is very different from your other work. It's very good, yes, very good, Miss James," Miss Kayte whispered.

"What is it you like about it?" My stomach snarled accompaniment to my words.

"I'm taken into the past when I look at her." Kayte held the sketch a distance in front of her and tilted her head back to view the painting. She set the sketch on the table, stepped backward, returned to it.

My heart echoed in my ears. My hands trembled. I felt again the same dream-like quality of the misty lilac-colored fog through which little Lulu and I walked hand in hand.

"We'll buy this sketch," Gilles blurted. His bushy eyebrows lifted.

I wondered if he'd spoken out of turn. Would Miss Kayte think him daft for buying my work so quickly? I knew the sketch wasn't worth much; I'd drawn it quickly and from memory. The piece was only pen and ink and a drop of watercolor, turquoise genuine here and there, and a hint of green to catch the child's eyes; merely an artist's ink rendering of a little girl in a park. If he paid me what I thought the sketch was worth I'd perhaps be able to buy a sandwich or a buttered baked potato and a foamy glass of beer from my bartender, Dave.

"What's your name again, Miss?" he asked. "Have I not seen you before? I think I've seen you somewhere, a number of years ago, perhaps?"

"Mister Gilles, she's Nyah James," Miss Kayte said. "We bought one of her paintings in Portland some years back."

"Why yes, of course. My memory isn't what it used to be. Miss James, here's what I can do. I'll buy the sketches of the child and of the park scene and I shall pay you . . . pay you, uh, would you please excuse Miss Kayte and me just for a moment?"

They stepped a mere twenty paces away. Miss Kayte's voice resounded an octave lower than Gilles's.

They strode over to me. Gilles said, "We would like to offer you twenty dollars for both sketches."

Twenty dollars for both of my sketches! I hadn't had twenty dollars in my pocket for, well, I couldn't remember since when. I felt I shouldn't jump up and down too quickly and take his offer, even though he wasn't a stupid man. He knew very well I was on the skids.

"Yes, I accept your offer. Thank you, Mister Gilles, Miss Kayte." I wanted to cry, but my tears had long since evaporated.

"No need to thank us, Miss James," Miss Kayte said. "We may have to thank you one day. By looking at paintings of landscapes, we never learn about the people who lived in the past."

Gilles softly coughed. "Miss James, let me tell you, let me give you advice. The world is full of landscapes, landscapes come into all galleries everyday by the dozens. Paint a portrait of the girl in the park. We'll buy it from you. In fact, we'll likely buy all of them you paint of her."

"Paint what you see, capture her innocence, her vulnerability, the secrets of her past hidden behind those sparkling turquoise eyes. She'll make you famous," Miss Kayte added, as she pulled two ten-dollar bills from her pocket purse.

With care, Mister Gilles tied my portfolio for me, led me to the front door, and out into the blur of snow and wind. "Where's your car, Miss James?"

"It's not too far of a walk," I stammered as I put on my gloves.

"But it's quite dark, my dear. It's not safe to be in the dark on this slippery road. I'm going to drive you home."

"No. I'll be fine. Good night, Mister Gilles, and thank you."

5
Beer-Battered Cod and a Stein of Beer!
Nyah

I arrived back at the Delmonico building with slant snow pounding my back and shivering in my worn-out boots. I shoved open the saloon door and slipped a bit on the wet floor. Immediately, the bells of pinball machines chimed, and the clank of pool balls striking each other made me smile. It was taco night. Dave, the owner of the building, was behind the bar gabbing and cajoling a half dozen cinnamon-haired men who were jostling each other, laughing, and sloshing beer down their throats.

"Hi Nyah, did you sell any of your work today?" Dave asked, walking toward me. "Let me take your coat," he added.

Smiling, I slipped off my coat and handed it over, stepped on the copper foot rail and perched myself onto a barstool, taking the load off my aching dogs. "Dave, please, I'd like your famous beer-battered cod and deep-fried chips and a lemon quarter. Oh, yes, and please, I'd like a nice head on my stein of beer. It's been a long time since I had a nice head of beer." My mouth was parched.

Dave smiled. He knew what this meant. "Congratulations! Beer-battered cod and the works," he called loudly across the room to the café.

"One order beer-battered cod, spud, tartar, and lemon," Mary shouted. "'It's about time ya sold a paintin', Nyah."

The high shrill tone of Mary's voice usually went through my head like a railroad spike, but I was too elated to care.

"And a nice head of beer comin' up," Dave said, grinning. "On the house." He set down the glass of Rainier in front of me, smiled, and walked back to the other end of the bar where he resumed talking to his regular patrons.

The saloon resembled any other: sienna-colored bar, faded pink bar stools, and the fifteen-foot-long beveled mirror on the wall behind showcased the entire room. The bar was scratched, grooved, and had rings and burn marks where men throughout the years had slammed down their beer mugs just before a fight was about to break out, where forgotten cigars and cigarettes fell out of the ashtrays while men were gossiping and telling fisherman's tales to anyone who'd listen.

On the other side of the tavern was the ten-stool diner where Mary, Dave's wife, stood at her grill most of the day and into the evenings. The first three buttons of her white short-sleeved blouse were unfastened, casting a moving shadow across her deeply blushing cleavage. A streak of silver parted her long chestnut hair down the middle, resembling a flash of lightning. The food-stained apron wrapped tightly around her tiny waist showed off her hour-glass figure. Mary could serve coffee, flip pancakes, fry bacon, scramble eggs, chat with her customers, and grill T-bone steaks with her spatula in one hand and her other hand scratching her left breast, all the while mindlessly chomping and snapping a stick of clove chewing gum.

Her freckled hawklike nose, which had a slight hook at the tip, was framed on either side by heavy-cast eyelids partially hiding olive-green eyes that glimmered like honey. Her thin lips, which sagged at the corners, were the same hue as her apricot-colored cheeks. Most days her hair was brushed back into a tractor-pull bun, around which she tied a jade-green bow. The tight hairdo accentuated her high cheekbones. My best guess was she was in her mid-thirties.

"Thanks, Mary," I said, while she placed a paper napkin and clanged a fork and knife down next to me.

"Ya betcha. And here's a coaster fer yer glass a beer. Sometimes Dave fergits the coaster."

I swiveled the stool seat and watched her glide back to her workstation, steady long strides, her hips straight, sensual movement coming from her sleek legs. Her shoulders were straight, thrown back and down, and her willowy neck held her head high. She wore white Converse High-Top sneakers with the bobbysocks turned down over them. The warm air, created by her swift pace, lifted her white A-frame skirt up to the back of her thighs. Her lengthy arms were loose, relaxed, swinging naturally. Never seeming in a hurry, it was as though she were savoring the movement of her body. The hypnotic sweet scent of clove gum lingered in her wake. Gaging her gait, I guessed her to be about six foot three, an inch or two taller than Dave.

"Nyah," Dave said. "Nyah?"

"Oh, Dave, sorry. I guess I drifted off."

"She's a pretty gal, isn't she?" Dave said, noticing me watching Mary walk away. "As I was saying, I'll pour a fresh head on your beer. Here comes your fish and chips." He returned to the other end of the bar with his patrons.

The spicy, tangy aromas drifting from the diner melded with the stale, acrid whiff of hazy cigarette smoke, causing my eyes to water. Onions, sizzling in butter, the spit of a T-bone steak hitting the hot grill, the clanging of dishes, the banging of pots and pans, the clinking silverware and the whistle of the teapot rose to a crescendo, and the fragrant brew of coffee, all together gave me an existential reason to keep on living.

"Want malt vinegar fer the fish?" Mary asked, setting the red and white checkerboard basket in front of me. "And here's some tangy coleslaw."

"Sure, I'd love some malt vinegar, and I love coleslaw. Keep what I owe you for my past due rent, plus for another week," I said, pushing my cash toward her. "And thanks for being patient with me."

"Sure, girl. Hey, ya comin' to our Hullabaloo Shindig tomorrow night?" Mary asked. "I'll be playin' ma fiddle and Dave'll be pluckin' his banjo, and we'll all be stompin' our feet and hootin' and hollerin'. I'm fryin' up chicken legs and whippin' up my homemade barbeque sauce, and there'll be bowls and bowls of peanuts and plenty of dancin'. Ya look like you need some fun, Nyah."

"What's a Hullabaloo Shindig?"

"Girl, you need to get out a lot more!" Mary said. "It's swing dancin'! We play music from Lionel Hampton's 'Boogie-Woogie' and

Glenn Miller's 'In the Mood,' to Bill Haley's 'Shake, Rattle and Roll' and 'See You Later Alligator.'"

"I can't dance," I said, my mouth watering over the aroma of my food.

"Then just come ta eat and stomp yer feet. Nyah, I promise ya won't be bored and you'll have lots a fun. It'll cheer ya up. And trust me, ya need cheerin' up."

"Well, sure. Okay. Sounds good." I savored my first crunchy bite of cod. Wiping the grease off my chin with a napkin, I added, "Yum, Mary. Your beer-battered fish is ambrosia."

"Eight o'clock tomorrow night then! I'll get a ta-go paper bag to take leftovers to your room, fer later, okay?"

"Thanks, Mary."

Dave and Mary had a wild shindig every Friday night. I knew that because my room was directly above the bar and I heard the laughter, the music, and the fun. Dave invited me a few times, but I never felt gay enough to be around crowds of folks. But I was warming up and my outlook was brighter.

Holding the red plastic basket on each side, I leaned down and wafted the steam into my nostrils. The scent of the dillweed and the tart lemon made my mouth pucker. I spread the red and white checkerboard paper open, and with my thumb and middle finger, picked up another piece of golden cod and dipped it into the zesty tartar sauce. As the hunk of fish neared my lips, I took in a breath of air, then blew on the fish a couple of times, parted my lips and bit into another juicy crunch of the catch of the day. I sipped a few gulps of Rainier and smiled at Dave after wiping my beer foam mustache from my upper lip. Dave winked at me.

6
Boogie-Woogie Hullabaloo
Nyah

After a chilling, unproductive day lugging my portfolio around in the ice wind, my shoulders slumped as I slipped and slid back to the Delmonico building. I rounded the corner of Water Street and my mood lifted as the muffled notes of banjos and fiddles and percussion and hearty laughter echoed off the tall stone buildings. I peeked through the large bay window facing the street. The bar was filled with smiling and grinning men and women, some sitting in chairs on the outer area of the dance floor, chomping on chicken legs, and still others were swinging and stomping and sliding over the floor, which was littered with peanut shells.

After I dropped off my portfolio in my room, I brushed my hair, brushed my teeth, and washed my face and hands. I took a couple of deep breaths hoping to gather enough courage to go downstairs and join the shindig. I pulled on my sweater and plugged in the space heater. Even though Mary always reminded me to turn off the light and unplug the heater when I wasn't there, this evening I felt like I deserved to return to a heated and lit up room. So I left the light switch on and made sure the heater was still radiating heat and shut the door behind me.

When I pushed open the saloon door, the blast of music, the foot stomping and the cigar and cigarette smoke put my head into a spin. I glanced around and found the table with the hot food and pitchers of cold beer and sat down nearby. The band was set up on an elevated stage in the back of the room. Downstage, the wind from the open back door was lifting the drummer's curly black hair around her head like a whirlwind. I recognized the piano player as a regular in the bar.

The fingers of a long-haired young man in a faded unbuttoned blue denim shirt were zipping across the frets of his electric guitar while at the same time he stomped his cowboy boots on the floor and blew into a harmonica hanging around his neck. An elderly lady wearing a black cowboy hat was sitting on a wooden crate, scraping a washboard with a fork. Dave, his wide-brim white cowboy hat cocked to one side, strummed and plucked his banjo, and Mary slid her rosin bow across the tightly wound strings of her fiddle. They were singing Duke Ellington's "Let's Get Together" at the front of the stage behind their microphones.

I was hungry. I piled a plate with crispy golden fried chicken legs, potato salad with bacon bits and pickles, a couple of mini sandwiches with ham and cheese, and two egg salad sandwiches. I poured a glass of Rainier from one of the sweating glass pitchers, making sure I piled a good head on it, and set my food and my glass of beer on the table which I'd reserved by drooping my jacket on the back of the chair. I devoured my juicy, crispy chicken leg in four bites then nibbled and sucked on the skin and bones, then I washed the yummy food down with a swig of beer. Then I poured a glass of Olympia into my mug. I liked both Rainier and Olympia beers. Drawn in by the wonderful sounds of joy, I bit into my second chicken leg while watching the crowd.

The men had a hand around the waists of the women, and the women were resting their left hand on the man's upper right arm, the other hands palm to palm, fingers intertwined. They were stomping their feet to the left then to the right, then flicked their toes forward then backward, then quickly tapping the tips of their toes, all the while swaying in the direction of each step.

Mary was stomping her pointed sienna and gray cowboy boots on the plank floor while plucking and strumming her fiddle upside down and backward from behind her head! *Woohoo!* shouted the crowd, joyfully clapping their hands. Mary's beautiful chestnut hair was flying every which way, and several strands of her silver streak were stuck to her sweaty cheeks and in the corners of her mouth. Dave was fingerpickin' and strumming his banjo to the breakneck beat of drums. I noticed I was stomping my rubber boots to the hoedown beat, and after another bite of chicken and a couple more chugs of beer, I shouted "Yahoo!" and cracked a smile.

I'd almost finished sucking on my last chicken leg when from across the room my eyes were held spellbound by a dazzling woman dancing with another woman. I'd never seen two women dancing together! Hand in hand they stepped quickly onto the middle of the dance floor and rocked side to side, backward and forward. One of them raised her arm so the other could make a full turn underneath. Then the other woman jumped high into the air, opened her legs, and fastened her thighs around her partner's waist so her pointed-toed cowboy boots were sticking straight up in the air!

Their bodies moved like one instrument, producing rhythms and sounds. Everyone in unison was shouting *"Yahoo!"* while clapping. The energy in the room was magical.

7
Buckskin Dancing
Nyah

Overnight the temperature dropped to thirteen degrees. Car batteries died. Engines stalled. Winds gusted. Tibbals Lake was locked in ice, delighting the town's ice skaters. The lashing snow entered houses through keyholes and under doors. My finger joints could barely grip my portfolio. At noon, I wrapped myself in my ragged jacket, wool hat, scarf, and gloves and staggered down the outside stairs to the bar, hardly able to clutch the splintered wooden handrail. Ice wind blew into my eyes, a shiver rolled over my shoulders like the incoming ice tide. Once inside the bar, a gigantic blast of wind slammed the heavy door shut behind me. Finally the warmth of the saloon surrounded me. I sat down on a stool farthest away from the door.

"Good morning, Nyah," Dave said, pouring a cup of coffee for me. "You look like something the cat dragged in, but last night you looked like you had a great time."

"The food was delicious. Being at your shindig was medicine for my spirit. You and Mary are so talented."

"You'd be surprised to know that our little town is known up and down the west coast for being an artist's town. And you can count yourself as one of us, now we've gotten to know you and your work."

"Thanks, Dave."

"Here, warm up those rickety bones of yours." He smiled and winked at me while he poured another cup of Hill's Bros. coffee. "Here's some honey and cream, or cane sugar, if you like. Let me take your coat."

"Take my coat? You want me to let you take my coat? You do know it's my only coat."

Dave pranced to my side of the bar. "Funny girl. Let me help you with your coat."

I obliged.

About twenty years back, Dave told me, he and Mary met at a powwow celebration put on by the Makah Indian Tribe at Cape Flattery, located on the very tip of the Olympic Peninsula. He told me she was the most beautiful Native maiden he'd ever seen and fell in love with her at first sight. Running Deer—her birth name—was taking part in her tribe's *Buckskin* dance. The powwow dance involved the Makah native maidens wearing crafted buckskin dresses with long cut leather strips which hung all the way to their ankles, and breastplates made from whale bone. Animal fur and bald-eagle tail feathers, decorated in handcrafted Indian bead designs of yellow, blue, red, green, raw umber and various shades in-between, hung from their hair. Each maiden decorated her own crown and hair barrettes, as well as her moccasins.

The maiden's dance was called *Buckskin Dancing* and was choreographed to be slow and poised while the dancers swayed and circled to the steady rhythm of the drums, knees slightly bent, bobbing to the beat, letting the long fringe on their sleeves sway in time with the drums, creating a beautiful effect of their leather fringe in a breezy motion. They carried beaded purses, swinging them as well, and their shawls, folded on an arm, swayed likewise.

Dave said he traded his favorite horse to her father in exchange for her hand in marriage.

"I hear coins jiggling in your coat pocket," Dave noted, while hanging my coat up on a wooden hook. "A wild guess is you need some hot breakfast this morning."

"Yes, yes, yes! Two eggs, scrambled, two slices of bacon, crispy, and some hash browns—with onions, please." Mary had left me a ten-dollar bill from the cash as change from my rent payment, so I had that much left to my name, enough left for a hot breakfast and coffee and a couple of dollars to give to the McGowen sisters for art supplies and still have cash in my pocket.

"Two eggs, beat 'em up, two toast, extra crispy, and give the hash browns some crunch—onions, side of ketchup," Dave ordered in a loud voice across the room.

"Comin' right up," Mary shouted, snapping her clove gum.

"I've been pretty cold," I said. "Sure wish I had a spare space heater."

"I know the owner," Dave whispered. "I'll get one in your room by the time you get back this afternoon. You'll sell another painting soon."

"Thanks, Dave. Can you make it two spare heaters? I accidentally busted the one I had. Sorry."

I wrapped both hands around the coffee cup to warm them. Savoring the aroma and every moment of the ceremony, I dripped golden honey into my coffee with a silver-plated teaspoon. From the white porcelain creamer, I poured fresh cream into the mixture and stirred. The strong aroma of the brew drifted up my nose and lifted my spirits. As I swallowed, I felt the nutrients of the cream, and the energy of the honey, and the heat of the coffee.

I watched Dave dry the glass beer steins with a crispy white towel. He held up each glass to the light to ensure no lipstick or fingerprints lingered on the rims. Then he stacked them upside down on a clean white bar towel. Above the beer mugs he stored the wine glasses by hanging them in a slot. He had two draft beer taps, one for Rainier beer and the other spigot drew Olympia beer. A gallon jug of pickled eggs sat next to a pile of white paper napkins and several mustard-yellow ashtrays stacked in the middle of the bar. Dave sold Camel cigarettes as well as Lucky Strikes, Old Gold, and Chesterfield, and Skoal chewing tobacco—Mary's favorite. A brass spittoon was on the floor opposite end of the bar from where I sat.

Dave understood I was a starving artist; in fact, he'd bought one of my oil paintings before the winter came upon the town. I knew he felt sorry for me because he offered me ten dollars for the twenty-four-by-twenty-inch painting, which I gratefully accepted. The painting was of his fifteen-foot oak bar with seven red-faced, bewhiskered

Irishmen—some sitting on the stools, others standing at the bar—each resting one foot on the brass footing. All the men had at least one hand on a glass of foamy cold lager. And, oh yes, a one-eyed dog they called Blinky, lying on the plank floor next to the brass spittoon. He'd hung the painting on the wall in back of the bar above the bar-length mirror.

Dave was a handsome man, about six feet tall, broad-shouldered, with phosphorescent light-blue eyes; a raw sexy guy, as far as guys go. A shock of nicely trimmed wavy blond hair barely touched the tips of his ears. A lock of his mane dangled halfway down his forehead in a little curl. His blue plaid Pendleton shirt, opened at the neck by three buttons and showing off his curly blondish chest hair, was tucked into his faded Levi blue jeans. With the sleeves rolled up to his elbows, the ringlets of hair on his lower arms glistened under the back-bar lights. His tight waistline was shown off by the burnt sienna cowhide belt with the big silver buckle, which he said he won at a bronco riding event back in his early twenties, about ten years ago.

He strode across the room to the walk-in cooler. A white hanky dangled out of his back pocket and swished in step with his stride. His shoulder blades rippled in rhythm and his hips moved like a cowboy's gait approaching his favorite horse, steady and self-assured. I liked his face, too, clean shaven, and he always smelled like English Leather cologne. Dave was a cowboy in every way.

"Here's yer breakfast, Nyah," Mary said, sliding the cream porcelain plate in front me. "Here's yer napkin. Now eat and git out there and sell some paintin's."

"Yeah, will do."

After I'd finished several cups of coffee, Dave winked at me again, while filling my green metal Thermos to the brim. He handed me a brown paper bag.

"Mary made you a baked turkey sandwich with mayo and cranberry sauce. She even tossed in a snappy dill pickle. Now get out there and sell your work. See you tonight, okay?"

"Okay. Thanks, Dave. Oh, and by the way, there were a couple of women at your hullabaloo last night, about my age, the taller one had blondish hair. Do you know her? She looked familiar to me," I lied, my face warming.

"Oh, you must mean Twiggy. Everyone knows Twiggy. She's the town reporter."

I tried not to show my interest in the woman, but as I turned away from Dave, I knew I had a twinkle in my eyes along with a grin on my face.

8
Alvena and Roseyl McGowen
Nyah

Fragrant essences of lavender buds and vanilla beans greeted me when I pushed open the heavy glass door to the Just as Good as It Used to Be Antique Boutique. A tiny bell rang above my head. A German-made Kieninger cuckoo clock, a reminder of the passing of each moment toward the grim reality of death, clicked the time away from the back of the store, a steady heartbeat, *tick, tock, tick, tock.* Every time the miniature cuckoo-bird popped out the wee yellow door, the faint echo of *cuckoo, cuckoo,* could be heard, a quiet prompt marking my days on earth.

"Well, hello dear," Miss Alvena McGowen said. "How are you?" She kissed my cheek.

"Miss Alvena, I've missed you." I hugged her warmly. "I'm feeling pretty good. I sold a couple of drawings to the Cape Flattery Art Gallery."

"Yes, we heard about your success in selling your work."

"They paid me twenty dollars. The first thing I did was treat myself to fish and chips at the One-Eyed Dog and a glass of Olympia. Now I've got a couple of dollars in my pocket, and I want to pay you for the art supplies from last month."

"Yes, our friend Kayte came for tea and told us all about your wonderful talent. She said you're gifted. And Nyah dear, we've always been happy to help you along with art supplies. They're our gifts to you."

Miss Alvena's fingers were long and bony. Her loose skin draped over the bones on the back of her hands and round blue veins rolled like twine down her long, sore-looking fingers. Her knuckles were bright red knots. Often, I'd seen her gently rubbing her knuckles. She was maybe five-foot-three and physically fit. Watermelon-colored hair heavily streaked with gray was brushed back on the sides and swept up on the back of her head. She might have been in her mid-eighties. Her face, nary a wrinkle, although she had smile lines in the corners of her twinkling blue eyes. Her reading glasses were perfectly round wire frames which she wore low on her nose. She wore pink shin-length pedal pushers and a cream-colored White Stag cardigan over a neatly pressed pink cotton blouse with the collar up in back. On her feet she sported a pair of black and white saddle shoes.

Her sister, Miss Roseyl McGowen, greeted us from the back of the store. "Yes! We'd hoped you'd come see us today," she said, warmly hugging me. Three times she kissed my cheek.

Miss Roseyl was about three inches taller than her sister. She wore a lovely shade of scarlet lipstick and sepia-colored mascara on the tips of her pink lashes. Her hair, powdered with yellow-gold tints and soft gray hues, was cut shoulder length with one side flipped up, like a white-cap in the sea. Her pear-green eyes burned right through me. Miss Roseyl's eyeglasses were the saturated color of sapphire. The McGowen sisters were Irish Twins, both born in the year 1870.

"You're just in time for a spot of tea." Miss Roseyl said, lowering her chin a half inch, peeking over her cream and taupe-colored eyeglasses, the top edges of which were decorated with wingtips.

"I smell orange blossoms and fresh honey," I said. "Some tea would be wonderful. Thank you."

The wooden plank floor creaked as we made our way to the quarter-sawn oak tea table in the back of the boutique. We nestled into our chairs at the round table. The sisters had spread on the table a crisp white linen tablecloth with bubblegum-colored embroidered edges. A large pear-shaped vase with two fresh long-stemmed apple-colored roses and many sprigs of lavender flowers sat in the middle of the table. Next to the lavender flowers was their lazy Susan which was filled with small, delicate finger sandwiches loaded with various cheeses and slices of ham, and some with slices of turkey and cranberries. A generous handful of raw lavender honeycomb, dripping fragrant honey onto the plate, still contained bee larvae. The sisters tended bees upstairs in the back of their attic. Three honeybees were closely circling the light-yellow comb. Cool cream, juicy lemon slices, fresh vanilla beans and jasmine buds, a basket of orange blossoms, and a branch of dewy green grapes were set around the table producing a colorful piece of art. Sterling silver teaspoons were on pink linen napkins.

Miss Alvena used one of the silver spoons to drop lavender and jasmine buds into our cups, then she poured steaming hot water over the flowers. Miss Roseyl, with her little finger pointing to heaven, daintily dropped a dash of cream into our cups, and with a teaspoon she dripped lavender honey into our cups. Miss Roseyl led us in a short prayer.

"Amen," I chimed in, stirring my tea. The chilled grapes beckoned me. I plucked a few.

Roseyl spoke. "Kayte said you painted sketches of a small girl you found sitting on a bench in the park."

"Yeah. She was holding a ragdoll in her arms. They want me to paint more of her, but the paintings were only sketches with some watercolors here and there. I'm not sure I can paint without a model. After I walked her to the orphanage, she simply and utterly disappeared."

"Orphanage? Disappeared? What do you mean?" Roseyl asked, glancing at Alvena.

"She vanished in a lilac-colored mist. I have little understanding of what happened to me in the park that night. The experience left me baffled. For now, I'll continue to paint whatever my imagination comes up with."

"What did she look like?" Alvena asked, giving Roseyl a long, unblinking look.

"Look like?" I asked, after swallowing the last of a turkey and cranberry finger sandwich. "She was only wearing a flour sack she said her mommy made her. There were honeybees embroidered into the dress."

"But what did she look like?" Roseyl insisted. "What color was her hair?"

"Strawberry. She looked like she was maybe five years old."

"And what do you mean, you walked her to the orphanage?" Alvena asked, again, giving her sister another long glance.

"She lived at the orphanage, at least that's what she told me. She put her hand in mine and pulled me along the lake, and when we arrived at the orphanage, she climbed up the stairs. Then she vanished, leaving behind the scarf and jacket and earmuffs I'd put on her."

"Then what did you do?" Roseyl asked, her voice sounding a bit shaky.

"I picked up her ragdoll and walked back to the Delmonico."

"What do you mean, you picked up her ragdoll?" Alvena asked.

"She dropped it before she crawled up the steps,'" I said, feeling a bit shaky myself. "Why are you two asking me these questions?"

"And what do you mean, she vanished?" Roseyl asked, ignoring my question.

"You two are scaring me." I pushed away my teacup.

"We're just trying to figure out what happened that night. How are you feeling after this encounter with this girl?" Roseyl asked. Again her voice was shaky.

"Unnerved. Nothing about that evening makes sense."

After the tea service, Alvena said, "Oh, wait a moment." She went behind the checkout counter and brought out a large sack. "Last week a man, a widower, came in and gave us his wife's unused painter's canvases. You have a lot of painting to do, dear, so here you go."

"Thank you. You're right. I'll need them. You two always have known what I need. I love you both. I don't know how I could've managed without you all these years."

"And we love you," Miss Roseyl said, waving her arm above her head.

9
My Name is Twiggy
Twiggy

I'd been home from New York City for three days when I decided to visit my friends who owned the Sequim Bay Restaurant just outside of town. I was tired and suffered from serious jetlag. I was driving my new Bullet-Nose Studebaker Champion coupe with the intention of staying on the road and not crashing into a snow hill.

My profession keeps me away from home many weeks a year. Don't get me wrong, I love my work, I meet nice people, and some not so nice people during my gigs. It's the long days of living in hotels—it rips apart my soul. I'm always lonesome, feeling separated from life, from like-minded women, but it's the life I'd worked toward since I was a wee tot. I'm not complaining, not really; I mean to say, sometimes I feel lost and homesick.

In my lifetime—I'm thirty-four—Port Townsend had never suffered such extreme winter, the winter of 1950. Everything was impenetrable with mountains of snow. The wind formed whitecaps on the shoreline of Port Townsend Bay, and after crashing onto the large boulders, the whitecaps froze instantly. The evening was arctic.

My headlights dimly lit up a person stumbling off to the far side of the crossroads. I slowed down and skidded to a stop. The nondescript figure wearing a black pea jacket magically reshaped into a woman all bundled up wearing a multi-colored ski cap and snow-packed rubbers up to her knees. I leaned over and rolled down the passenger side window.

"You need a ride?" I asked her.

She slipped over to my car, poked her head in the window, looked into my eyes and said, "I could, indeed."

"Well, hop in."

The lady opened the passenger door and slid over the seat. "What are you doing walking in the dark on a night like this?"

"I thought I'd treat myself to a nice dinner," she said. "I heard the Sequim Bay Restaurant has good food. It's outside of town. Is Discovery Bay out of your way?"

"No, not at all," I said. "As a matter of fact, I'm on my way to the restaurant to have dinner myself. What a coincidence. Will you be meeting a friend?" I'd hoped she'd say no.

"No. Are you meeting a friend?"

"No, and I don't believe in coincidence, not the way people define the word. By the bye, my name's Twiggy Carpenter. And who are you, my little frozen friend, if you don't mind my asking?"

She said her name was—and I quote— "Nyah, Nyah James."

My first glance toward Nyah, Nyah James, took in baby-blues that had a deep purple ring around each iris, and the tips of her eyelashes were frosted white. Each time she blinked another snowflake dripped onto her lap. Her flushed cheeks highlighted her alabaster skin and the daring splash of freckles across her nose and cheeks. Her eyelids lazily covered the top third of her eyes, which to me was very sexy. She had an easy, lighthearted way about her. Her grin was soft, no teeth showing, an easy lift on the corners of her mouth. The moment she sat in the passenger seat she took off one glove and smoothed her hand slowly over my leather car seat.

"I sold two paintings to the Cape Flattery Art Gallery," Nyah said. "Well, not actual paintings. A couple of pen-and-ink sketches. One was of a little girl I'd met in the park the other night, and the other a pen-and-ink sketch of the park itself. The gallery manager liked them so much he bought them both for twenty bucks. Twiggy? Where'd you get your name? Very unusual. I like it."

"My grandmother's mother was a carpenter during the Civil War. And her specialty was building miniature dollhouses. My grandmother worked as a forest ranger during World War II. Thus, my grandmother made up her own name, Twiggy Carpenter, a sort of play on words. Would you like to have dinner together?"

"Sounds good. I could use a hot Grand Marnier for starters. What about you?"

"A hot Grand Marnier sounds fine," I said. "How long have you been painting? Would I know any of your work?"

"I doubt it. I've been drawing and painting since I could pick up a brush. What is it you do? Wait a moment, come to think of it—Twiggy Carpenter—your name sounds familiar. Or maybe I had a dream or something."

"My family owns and operates the *Gazette* down by the marina on Water Street. Mum's the editor and Granny, the owner, carries a big stick but speaks softly. I've been working as the in-house reporter since high school. So, you think you may have dreamed about me?"

"Yeah. You're a reporter and you also write the editorial column. I don't know how come I think this, but didn't you graduate from the University of Washington? Or maybe I dreamed you did."

Nyah blushed. My own face felt warmer by the second. "Ha, funny lady. You must read the *Gazette*. Yes, in 1932, after graduating college with my degree in journalism, I came home and continued writing for the paper. Wait a moment. Nyah, Nyah James. Granny bought one of your landscapes this last summer at your one-woman show. The painting's hanging in her home studio. No kidding, she really did."

"Are you sure you didn't dream Granny bought one of my paintings?"

"Yes, I'm sure. You painted it from the point of view of Fort Casey across the Strait of Juan de Fuca to the hundred-foot bluff on North Beach. You painted the sea with high white caps crashing against the shore at the bluff, and one lonely sailboat fighting the storm. I fell in love with it. Granny teased me and hasn't given it to me to this day."

My impression of Miss Nyah, Nyah James, was she had no idea how sexy she was. My heart raced. And I fell in love, totally.

10
I Can Dream, Can't I?
Nyah

I'd been hungry, cold, and lonesome for so long, having a few dollars in my pocket renewed my belief that I might be able to make a living as an artist. All I'd ever dreamed of was being a real artist, to have my name known in the field of art, to be among the biggies. I woke up with the need to tell the world I was doing well as an *artiste*. So, I decided to treat myself to a fine, steaming hot dinner.

The town had no taxi service, so I bundled up in my coat, gloves, boots, and my hat of many colors, and plodded down Water Street. Several blocks later, at the far end of town, I heard iron tire chains crunching into the deep, frozen snow. A Bullet-Nose Studebaker Champion skidded up beside me and slipped to a stop. I poked my head halfway inside her window. The dome light inside her car gave off enough light to see she looked to be my age, I'm thirty-two. Her eyes looked to be the color of lavender, and her titanium hair was cut in the ducktail style, with curly bangs. Those curly bangs got under my skin; the stars drifted out of the sky and tickled my heart. She asked me if I wanted a ride. I tingled when I saw her smile.

She stretched and opened the door from across the seat and I jumped in. The Andrew Sisters were singing, "I Can Dream, Can't I?" on her radio. She said her name was Twiggy Carpenter.

Miss Carpenter was wearing soft cream-colored wool slacks and a pink long-sleeve silk blouse with folded up cuffs at the wrists and a lovely, lavender floral design scarf draped over one shoulder. Her shoes were rich-looking brown leather penny loafers worn with white bobby socks. Her baubles and bangles—diamond earrings, sterling bracelet, and a gold watch—added to the impression she was well-off. Even her full-length white rabbit coat, which drooped over the back of the front seat, looked as though no thought had gone into how it slumped. If I had to put her appearance into one sentence it would be, she carried herself with the air of casual elegance.

What luck, I thought. I had a bit of money clinking in my pocket and a warmth flooded over me. I felt I'd met the woman I was going to spend the rest of my life with. A lovely lady, with long red fingernails and lipstick to match, had asked me to have dinner with her.

The snow on my coat and hat battled with the warm air of the coupe. Evidence of the clash became apparent when the inside windows quickly fogged the view. Miss Carpenter flipped a button on her dashboard and warm air quietly blasted out, evaporating the sweat of the windshield. Within moments, the inside of her car held the fragrance of Chanel Number Five, which filled my senses. The two-lane road was packed with snow and the four-foot snowdrifts had frozen on both sides of the road. The windshield wipers kept the windows clear of the large snowflakes, but the horizontal blowing flurries made it difficult to see the road. The back-and-forth motion of the blades sent me into a hypnotic spell.

The Sequim Bay Restaurant parking lot was vacant, silent, but the *Open* sign hung by twine on the inside of the door. Twiggy pushed up the column gearshift into the park position and set the foot brake. She left the windshield wipers swooshing back and forth.

""You ready to bundle up?" she asked, as she reached for her fur coat. In so doing her fingers touched my hand. Goosebumps prickled up the nape of my neck.

"Oh, excuse me, Nyah," she said. "I didn't scratch you with these fingernails, did I?"

"No, not at all."

"Say, your face is a bit flushed," Twiggy said. "Are you okay?"

"Sure."

She draped her fur coat over her lovely broad shoulders. I pulled on my gloves. The wind howled making it a bit difficult to push open the door of the Bullet-Nose. Once Twiggy was successful in getting her car door open, she reached her fur-lined, leather-gloved hand to me and I reached back. She helped me slide my way across the seat to the open door, and let the wind slam the door behind me.

"Be careful, Nyah. I want you to stay on your feet! Oh, no, the lavender sprigs in your hat blew away!"

"I can get more."

11

I'm A Ghost by Nature
Nyah

"Well, hello there, Twiggy," a woman said after a little bell rang above the door. "How you been?"

"Hi Suzie. I've been well, thank you. It's so nice to see you again. And how have you been?"

"I'm very well, thank you. We were excited when you called for a reservation. We haven't seen you for a while."

"I've been out of town for a couple weeks," Twiggy said. "I get pretty tired being on tour weeks at a time."

"I bet your mother's happy to have you back at the paper."

"Suzie, I'd like you to meet my friend, Nyah, Nyah James," Twiggy said deflecting from the comment about her mother.

"So nice to meet you, Nyah," Suzie said. "Twiggy, let me hang up your coat. Oh, Nyah, let me hang up yours, too."

Recognizing her offer as an afterthought, I hurriedly slipped off my scarf and gloves and tucked them into the pocket of my ratty coat and handed it and my cap to Suzie. I combed my fingers over my ponytail, hoping to slick down stray hairs. I realized how homeless I appeared and felt my face blush. I was wearing a pair of old blue jeans with holes in each knee, and a blue blouse with crimson and yellow paint stains near the neckline. Covering the blouse was a beige wool button-up cardigan I'd bought at the second-hand store for a dime. When Suzie lumbered to the coatrack, I noticed her left hip had a pronounced limp. The sway of her right hip rose about two inches higher than the left. She softly petted Twiggy's fur coat and rubbed the collar on her cheek. While molesting Twiggy's fur coat, she dropped my rag on the floor, but quickly picked it up with her thumb and index finger, as if it might be infested. I pretended not to notice.

"Would you like your usual table, Twiggy?" Suzie grabbed two menus.

"Yes, by the fire."

"May I start you ladies off with a drink or a glass of wine?" Suzie asked, setting our menus on the table next to the crackling fireplace.

I sat down quickly to hide my rubbers under the table, then hung my purse, which held what was left of my fortune, on the back of my chair. "I'd like a hot Grand Marnier in a wide snifter, please," I said, my face still warm from the embarrassment of my raggedy coat.

"I'd like the same. And thanks, Suzie," Twiggy said, setting her clutch purse on the table next to her menu.

"Coming right up," Suzie said and walked away.

"Do you have family, Twiggy?" I asked, then felt as if my question might be too personal. After all, I'd only known her for a moment in time. "I hope you don't mind me asking."

Before Twiggy could answer, Suzie came back to our table and set white cloth napkins off to the side and gently placed two forks on each, one fork shorter than the other, next to a spoon and dinner knife. Then she walked away and returned with a glass of water for each of us.

"Of course I don't mind you asking about family," Twiggy said. "I want to get to know more about you, too. Yes, I have a family. I work with my mum at the *Gazette*. She's my boss, and she's good at what she does. And she never lets me forget it."

"What do you mean?"

"Mum believes journalism is one of the most important careers a woman can have. According to her, being an artist or a musician is self-indulgent and a waste of time. But I love music. So, in graduate school I majored in journalism and minored in music, just to piss her off."

"I bet she's proud of you, though."

"She hasn't had any complaints about my work at the paper, which makes her happy, I guess."

Suzie returned and set down our drinks. "Tonight, our special is our meatloaf, your choice of a baked potato or mashed. Fresh string beans and a Caesar salad comes with it."

I looked at Twiggy and she looked at me and smiled. My vagina pinged.

"Nyah, how does the meatloaf special sound to you?" Twiggy asked, while handing the menus back to Suzie. "I promise it's very tasty."

"Okay, sounds great. I'd like the potatoes mashed."

"Suzie, could you serve us your famous meatloaf special in, say, a half hour or so please? We'd like your homemade biscuits right away, with butter, of course. I'd like the potatoes mashed, too."

"Of course. Enjoy each other."

"You sure are tall, Twiggy. You carry yourself well," I commented. "Actually, you're really a beautiful lady."

"Thank you, Nyah. I'm six feet tall."

"What did you mean when you told Suzie you've been on tour?"

"Let's talk about that at another time, okay, Nyah?"

"Sure, another time."

This woman named Twiggy was looking into my eyes and into my soul. I squirmed. I'm a ghost by nature—although being a ghost is a lonely life. I was painfully self-conscious being in the company of Miss Twiggy Carpenter, a woman so polished in appearance. Everything about her was elegant. Her ducktail haircut was the cutting-edge style of 1950, and a bit risqué. The style was called a ducktail in polite company, and nicknamed the DA, which stood for the duck's-ass haircut, among friends.

Twiggy crossed her legs and set her white linen napkin on her lap. I copied her and attempted to cross my legs, but my boots were a tad too big and wouldn't fit between the leg of the table and my chair.

I wondered where Twiggy bought her wardrobe, surely not at JC Penney's or the Newberry's dime stores on Water Street. Even her penny loafers looked too expensive for Penney's. There I sat with the most intriguing, captivating woman I had ever seen or spoken to in real life. She looked like the movie star, Lana Turner.

In comparison, my dishwater-reddish ringlets stretched back in a ponytail—a PA, pony's ass—with a green cotton scarf wrapped around the rubber band. My pallid skin was in all likelihood a bit shiny from the layer of Pond's Vanishing Cream rubbed into my cheeks, which I'd smoothed on to keep my face from cracking. I was Cinderella before the ball.

"I come from a long line of newspaper women," she told me. "As I said, I'm a reporter and a trained observer, and yes, I do have a bit of intuitive mind-reading as part of who I am."

Suzie set our biscuits and butter in front of us. She sat down with us, on the edge of a chair.

"So, where you from, Nyah?" Suzie asked.

"That's a good question. I'm not sure of much about my childhood. It's a blur. I've been told I was orphaned as a small girl."

"Orphaned? Really?" Twiggy asked, after sipping the Grand Marnier.

"I had no family after my mother disappeared. Miss Roseyl from the antique store told me I'd lived in the woods, scrounged for food from garbage cans, begged for nickels and dimes until someone noticed me—or so I'm told."

My nerves rattled. I was talking too fast. I didn't actually know anything about my life when I was a child, other than what information the McGowen sisters shared with me. And I never asked them to tell me more. I took my first gulp of hot Grand Marnier. Whew, it burned all the way down my throat and sizzled inside my empty stomach. The gulp made my eyes water. I drank deeply of several ounces of cold water.

"How long have you two known each other?" Suzie asked, pretending not to notice my puddling tears.

"I picked up this pretty lady along Water Street," Twiggy said. "She was walking from town to treat herself to one of your famous dinners.

She's a talented artist and has several of her paintings hanging in galleries from Seattle to Whidbey Island, to Port Angeles, Discovery Bay, and Port Townsend, oh yes, and in Portland, Oregon as well. She's a very gifted painter, indeed."

Twiggy had no idea if I had art in galleries or not. She only knew her grandmother had bought one of my paintings a while back. But suddenly, her description of me explained my eccentric appearance— I was an artist.

"How nice! What's your name again, dear?"

My face burned. "Nyah, Nyah James. How do you and Twiggy know each other?" I asked, switching the attention away from myself.

"Oh, the whole town knows about Twiggy," Suzie said. "Her family's been living in Port Townsend for generations. In fact, her mother was our longest running mayor. She runs our newspaper, as well."

"Really? I'm impressed, Twiggy. Your mother sounds like the pillar of the town."

Twiggy abruptly shifted her position in the chair.

"Is there something wrong?" Suzie asked. "Twiggy, you okay?"

"What? Oh, no, everything's great. Yes, Mum's a pillar. Mum runs everything. Suzie, please bring me another hot Grand Marnier, this time in a hot mug."

"Sure. Right away." She rose and hastened off.

Twiggy's face had turned ashen. I took another sip of Grand Marnier, which burned down my throat. We remained silent.

"Here you are, Twiggy," said Suzie, quickly setting the hot mug near her plate.

Twiggy sipped the hot drink straight away.

"Say, Nyah, my husband—" Suzie said, "well, he's always wanted a nice painting of our restaurant. Would we be able to commission you to do a painting of our building? Or maybe you'd paint a mural of the inside of our restaurant and its décor? It'd be a nice addition for us, for posterity, being in this historic building and all."

"Thank you and I accept. I can begin next week. I'm very excited. Actually, I'm speechless."

Suzie and I shook hands. When Suzie limped away, I looked at Twiggy. "Twiggy, a penny for your thoughts."

Twiggy winked at me. My heart felt like a bowl full of Jell-O. To be in her company, to talk about life and other magical things without having to think about the point of my existence and wonder why I descended to the planet Earth in the first place, dumbfounded me.

"I'd like to make a toast," Twiggy said, smiling.

We raised our glasses together. "I want to give thanks to the universe that Nyah, Nyah James strolled into my life tonight, right into a friendship with me."

We wrapped our elbows together and sipped our drinks.

"I'm flattered, Twiggy. I feel the same way."

Twenty minutes later Suzie and her husband arrived at our table, each carrying our meatloaf specials. The pair looked to be about sixty-five years old. His face was round, his cheeks flushed, and his hair was in various stages of male-pattern baldness. His wide smile stretched across his face showing off his slightly crooked white teeth.

"Roger, this is Miss Carpenter's new friend, Miss Nyah James. Nyah, I'd like you to meet my husband of forty-five years. I told him you agreed to paint a mural of the inside of our restaurant, and he couldn't be happier."

"I'm looking forward to it," I told him.

Roger bent down and gave Twiggy a kiss on each cheek. "How's your mother?"

"She's fine." Twiggy pushed her potatoes around on her plate, stabbed a piece of meatloaf, pushed it into the pile of potatoes and gravy and put the bite into her mouth.

"Twiggy, are you okay?" I asked.

"You do look a little peaked," Suzie said.

"A little jetlag, probably," Twiggy said.

"Roger, give her the money, dear."

"Yes," Roger said to me, "you'll want money for paint and large brushes and anything else you'll need. If you need more than ten dollars to buy supplies, let me know right away. Oh, and here's a ten upfront for all your work."

"Roger, give her those photos," Suzie ordered. "We found some original photos of our restaurant dating back to the1920s. We thought you could get ideas from how it looked in here back in the day."

Roger handed me the cash. My first thought was I was going to get a modern haircut, perhaps a DA, with my newly acquired fortune and spend some time in JC Penney's looking for some updated slacks, blouses and sweaters, and perhaps a bottle of perfume. My second thought was to stock my rickety old refrigerator with food.

"Roger and I will leave you two alone now," Suzie said. "We hope you enjoy getting to know each other. Let me know if you'd like another drink."

"Thank you both," I said, fervently.

Watching Twiggy eat fascinated me. I kept a close eye on what utensils she used for what food. When she picked up the small fork, I picked up my small fork and waited to see what food on the plate Twiggy would eat first. She started with the salad. I was eager to learn how to eat using proper manners. When she looked up at me, I quickly looked down into my salad. But I'd noticed she stabbed the salad with the prongs of her short fork pointing down into the salad and inserted the fork with the salad on it between her lips and into her sexy mouth. I copied her.

After a couple of bites, she lifted the napkin from her knee, and gently, with the corner of the linen, dabbed the corners of her mouth, before replacing the napkin back onto her knee. I copied her, except when I tried to put the napkin back onto my knee it fell to the floor. I slid it under my chair with my boot.

"It's sexy and quite edgy the way you use a fork," I said.

"So, you think I'm sexy?" she asked, after setting down the short fork and picking up the longer one and stabbing a piece of meatloaf, then scooping a bit of mashed potatoes on top of the meatloaf with the prongs pointing down, then putting the loaded fork in her mouth.

I stabbed a piece of meatloaf and scooped a bit of mashed potatoes on top of the meatloaf with the prongs pointing down and popped the fork into my mouth, almost missing my mouth. I was embarrassed to be so transparent.

"Why Nyah, I do believe I've embarrassed you," Twiggy teased.

"You were saying your mother's good at what she does," I reminded her.

"She has several journalism awards including the Pacific Northwest Excellence in Journalism, which she was awarded when she was teaching at the Graduate School of Journalism at the University of Washington. At age forty-five, she won a Pulitzer Prize as a newspaper correspondent during the Dust Bowl of the 1930s. My dad passed twenty years ago. Mum and her long-time companion live together on the other side of Discovery Bay. He's retired from the lumber mill. Spends a lot of time in the bars. I can see their house when I look through my sea captain's telescope, which I do on occasion."

"You spy on your mum through a sea captain's telescope?"

"Not really," Twiggy said, smiling. "I wanted to see if you were listening to me."

"What happened to your dad?"

"Back in the thirties the Great White Plague was rapidly spreading," Twiggy said. "It was known as consumption. Today doctors call it tuberculosis. Dad started coughing up blood. We admitted him to a sanatorium in Arizona. Doctors decided to collapse his infected lung which resulted in his death. I'm really hungry. I'm going to order more biscuits and gravy."

"Wow, we went from your dad's collapsed lung to 'I'm hungry let's order more biscuits and gravy.'"

Twiggy swallowed several sips of her Grand Marnier and didn't reply right away. "My mum's mother, who I call Granny, was also a journalist and taught at the Graduate School of Journalism at the U of

Washington. Granny covered Amelia Earhart's solo flight across the Atlantic. She witnessed—in person, I might add—Earhart's landing on the twentieth of May, 1932, in a pasture in Northern Ireland. Granny became instant friends with Earhart, and later she met and became good friends with Eleanor Roosevelt, another close friend of Earhart's. Granny and Mum have owned the *Gazette* since 1918. Granny's eighty years young. She and her partner have been together for fifty-five years. They live on the bluff at North Beach overlooking the Strait of Juan de Fuca."

I heard all this with great interest. "Do you have any brothers or sisters?"

"No, I'm the surviving child. And no, I've never been married, and I have no children," added Twiggy, as an afterthought. "My younger brother, Gus, was killed in 'forty-two in the Second World War. He was twenty-one." Twiggy swallowed another sip of her drink.

"Oh, dear, I'm so sorry."

Suzie came over and asked if we were enjoying the meatloaf.

"The meatloaf is delicious, Suzie," Twiggy said.

After Suzie walked away, Twiggy said, "After Gus was killed by a German kamikaze, my younger sister, Katie Jo, moved to Britain and joined the Women's Timber Corps. She felt a need to join the war effort, and the Corps was the only war entity hiring women to work in forestry."

"The Woman's Timber Corps? I've never heard of it."

"During the war Great Britain hired women to work the forests, cutting down trees, working the horses and all. The winter was bad in 'forty-three. According to the death certificate, Sis and her friend were driving in an area in Yorkshire. The blizzard was raging, and they drove their '38 Ford into a deep snowdrift. When authorities found them, the car was covered with ice and snow. My sister and her girlfriend, Patch, smothered inside the cab of the car. She was twenty-three."

"Oh, my God, I am so sorry."

The corners of her mouth drooped. She stared into the fire without blinking. Her eyes watered profusely from what I figured was drinking her hot drink so quickly.

She pushed her meatloaf around the plate. Still, she stared into the fire.

"Twiggy? Where are you? Twiggy?"

"How about you?" Twiggy mumbled. "Have you been married? Do you have family?"

"Twiggy, there's something wrong with you. What is it?"

"Just a bit of jet lag. Tell me a bit about yourself. I do want to know."

I decided not to ask her why she thought she was suffering the effects of jetlag. "I've never wanted to be married. I've always wanted to paint, to be an artist. Aren't you hungry?"

Distracted, her gaze darted aimlessly around the restaurant. Quite abruptly, Twiggy's breath became labored. Her lips quivered. She dropped her fork into her mashed potatoes and clutched her chest. Her hands were shaking.

"Twiggy! Are you choking? Twiggy, what's the matter?"

"I have to get out of here."

She shoved back her chair, swayed back and forth as she made her way across the room, pushed open the exit door, and ran into the frightful blizzard. Frantically, I went after her, out into the snowdrifts.

12
The Rolling Pin
Twiggy

I'd fallen into a snowdrift face down. I remember, vaguely, hearing muted voices shout my name—*Twiggy, Twiggy*.

I remember the heavy weight of coldness surrounding me and pinning me down. I was blind, and a strong sensation of suffocation overwhelmed me. My thoughts were of my sister. And that I was trapped—smothered.

I came out of my blackout in front of a blazing fire, bundled from head to toe in several blankets. Nyah and Suzie were on either side of me. My heart hammered against my chest. My eardrums vibrated at a high-octave pitch. My fingers and toes tingled frightfully with nerve pain. Melting snow dripped into my eyes, causing a fire-burning sensation. I shivered violently. I was hiccupping.

Suzie held a hot mug of Grand Marnier to my lips. I felt the heat between the palms of my unsteady hands. Nyah had her arm around me, holding my head on her shoulder. About forty-five minutes later, my respiration slowed, and I felt my spirit spread throughout my body.

Forty-five minutes was the usual amount of time it took for my terrifying panic episodes to subside. For most of my life, these attacks have ambushed me from out of nowhere. My first episode was the night before my first day of kindergarten. The month was September, the year was 1919, I was age four and a half, and the time was midnight. I'd woken up and found myself aimlessly walking along a dirt road in my pajamas. The road was surrounded by trees and blackberry bushes. Darkness engulfed me. I was shaking fiercely. I was barefoot. I was alone. And I was scared out of my wits. I screamed and cried. The more I screamed, the faster my heart raced.

Mum found me. She spanked me for wandering around at night in my pajamas. Mum tanned my hide often. Once she pushed me so hard I landed on the kitchen floor. She slowly approached me and randomly kicked me several times. When she stopped her attack, we stared into each other's eyes. I'd concluded I was a bad little girl. Throughout the years I'd wake up screaming and hiccupping from terrifying nightmares. Mum would be shaking me. When I came out of the trance, I told Mum that in my dream, she was beating me with a rolling pin. Mum slapped my face and told me never to tell anyone about the rolling pin. I never did.

Getting to know Nyah in a restaurant where everyone knew me—knew I'm the daughter of the town's prominent newspaper woman—filled me with anxiety, afraid my mum would find out I had dinner with a woman. I'm embarrassed to say all I learned about Nyah during our first dinner together was that she was an orphan who ended up living in the woods begging for money and eating out of garbage cans. I was so involved in my shame about loving women, my soul went on hiatus—I checked out—wasn't fully present. I'm afraid my anxiety got the better of me. And I had too much to drink.

13
Skating with Little Lulu
Nyah

It was one of the days of winter beauty for which Port Townsend was known. Indigo blue sky with whipped white clouds moving slowly in from the Strait of Juan de Fuca. The windows of the Victorian homes glimmered; the icy rooftops flickered. Television antennas were heavy-laden with snow and the homey scent of smoke from white hickory drifted from chimneys of the beautiful uptown homes. Chevrolets, Fords, and big-finned Studebakers were parked perfectly in driveways or inside the detached garages of the Victorian estates.

Tibbals Lake was frozen solid. From as far away as Discovery Bay came skaters, and I was no exception. I sat on a bench near the shore and laced up the boots of my scruffy leather skates. When I stood, my ankles wobbled. I stepped off the edge onto the frozen lake and skated in a wide circle. The powder snow sifted into the cold air and the sun warmed my cheeks.

To warm up my stiff winter joints, I bent my knees, stuck out my rump and wiggled it side to side. I fell right away. Every skater knows when you're going to fall, you may as well go with the fall, if for no other reason than to save the pink face of embarrassment. So I bent my knees a tad and with deliberation landed on my rear, which did not have much padding. I rolled over on all fours, picked up one leg, and put the skate blade back on the ice. I proceeded in the same manner with the other blade until I was gliding upon the ice again. I felt I had to prove myself to anyone who may have been laughing at me, so I circled three times, stopped for a moment with my free foot extended behind me, swung my free leg forward and around with a wide scooping motion, jumped in the air and landed backwards. I must have been warmed up because I didn't fall again.

I pushed off in a long stride across the ice, taking deep breaths. The fresh air and my newly found self-confidence made me feel healthy and strong. I felt my blood gushing swiftly through my veins, and the fresh, cold air on my face was absolutely invigorating. Women and men, hand in hand, crossed my path. Children flashed past me, bent over, cutting ice and wind. An elderly woman with an orange woolen scarf around her neck was doing fancy choreographed figures. She swung forward, jumped, and circled backward, skates together, knees bent, intent and proud. All around me was the quiet flow of skaters moving and gliding, the creaking sound of steel on ice, the cold air, and soft laughter.

But the neighborhood looked a bit queer to me. The lake, the surrounding trees and the white winter ducks seemed strange, surreal, like thin gauze, as if a barely visible screen were wrapped around all my skin. The slant snow stopped. My ears popped, dulling my hearing.

I saw Lulu.

Wearing a dark long dress, a short dark coat, and a pair of white boots onto which were attached to old-fashioned wooden skates, she was making a figure-eight look easy. She seemed quite a bit taller than when we were together only a few weeks ago, and her face looked older, and she looked to be about nine years of age. Perhaps she wasn't Lulu at all, but another young girl who looked like her.

She looked up at me. Our eyes met. With a wide smile, she skated to my side and pressed her toe into the ice to hold herself in place.

"Hello, Miss James," she said.

"I thought I saw you skating, but you look older than the last time we were together."

She gently grasped my hand in hers. "Let's skate!"

But still the mist swirled. The women and men and children skated silently. My own breath and the light laughter coming from Lulu as she guided me around the lake were the only sounds I heard besides our own quiet motions, all of which brought me back to the feeling I had the first time I met Lulu: of being in a dream, yet still not being in a dream.

"You noticed I'm older since we last were together."

I smiled.

Lulu said, "I want to catch up to you, do you understand? As you know, I'm not mindful of time. I keep growing up and growing up."

"Are you my little dream?" I asked. "I feel I'll soon wake up and you'll be gone again."

"Where do you live?" she asked. Her voice sounded grown up, too.

"In a room at the Delmonico building down on Water Street, but I hope to be moving soon. I drew a sketch of you the day after we met in the park. I sold it to a gallery. They liked the sketches so much they said they'd buy more portraits from me."

"How wonderful," Lulu said, enthusiastically.

"Oh, and the owners of the Sequim Bay Restaurant commissioned me to paint a mural of their restaurant. The job will keep me in money for a good amount of time and who knows, I may get more painting commissions. Maybe I'll buy a house. You brought me luck, little Miss Lulu."

Her hand clasped mine as we skated around the lake. Her long skirt flared out when she let go of my hand and executed a twirl. She skated with such ease, crossing her right foot over the left, her left foot over her right.

"Who'll the portraits be of?" she asked, again grasping my hand. "Will you paint them of me? I know they'll be of me. I'm going to have pictures of me painted and hung in a gallery for all to see."

"I also met a very nice lady. I was slipping and sliding down Water Street in the snow on my way to buy myself a nice dinner with the money the gallery owners paid me. The lady felt sorry for me. She drove me to the restaurant, and we had a nice evening together."

Abruptly, Lulu let go my hand and skated off by herself. I was perplexed.

She fell on her backside and sat there on the ice. I coasted over to help her stand. Her face was flushed, and she wouldn't look up at me. She seemed lost in a dream as though in another time, looking off into the distance toward the orphanage.

"Would you like a nice cup of hot chocolate?" I asked. "There's a small vendor booth at the edge of the lake."

Lulu seemed in a better frame of mind when I mentioned cocoa. With girlish glee, she said, "Yes! I would love a cup of hot chocolate!"

This time I took her hand in mine, and we soon sat together on a park bench holding our steaming paper cups of chocolate. The scent of the hot steam filled my senses. The elderly woman skater in the orange neck scarf sat near Lulu and me. The chilly air smelled like the inside of Dave's beer cooler. The wet leather skates and the damp wool of the elder woman's orange scarf gave me a headache.

"Are you still at the orphanage?" I asked.

"Yes, I'm still at the orphanage. Where else would a parentless girl of nine be?" She added, "We're studying the Great Depression and the Dust Bowl."

"How's your sister, Annie?"

Lulu stared toward the lake. I presumed she was watching the skaters until her bottom lip quivered. She took a quick sip of chocolate. I was unsure if I should ask her why she was crying. Lulu seemed a gentle soul, an older soul. I wanted her to know I cared about her.

"Lulu, why are you crying? Are you hungry?"

She raised her paper cup to her tiny mouth, but she didn't drink. Instead, she wrapped her palms around the cup and sniffed the sweet chocolate steam. Perhaps she was being neglected at the non-existent orphanage. She looked up at me, the cup of chocolate still in her palms—her turquoise eyes—puddles of warm water.

"Annie died."

"Oh dear, Lulu." I wrapped my arm around her shoulders and held her close. "I'm sorry, my dear."

In a singsong voice she said, "Sometimes the black dust and sand blow through the air so hard it causes static electricity so bad my scalp tingles, and my hair stands on end, like barbed wire. Sometimes when I touch metal the static electricity knocks me on my bottom. Sometimes at night the horns of the cattle glow. Everything dies of suffocation. The mountains of dirt and gravel kill everything. Mother rubs Vaseline in our noses to try to keep us from breathing the dust, but nothing stops the dust."

"Lulu, the Dust Bowl was during the 1930s. I don't understand."

"Miss James, I told you before, time means nothing to me."

There was something very peculiar about sitting next to Lulu, drinking chocolate together. I couldn't shake the feeling I was in a dream, but the hot paper cups we held in our hands said otherwise. The tears in Lulu's eyes and her quivering, tiny lips were real, and it all was the truth. I still had her ragdoll back in my studio, and that was the truth. All the same, I felt strange, as though she didn't belong, like we were living in different times from each other. I have no other way to say how I felt except to say I felt off, dissociated from everything and everyone, except while being with her. At the same time, it seemed very right for us to be sitting on a park bench next to the lake watching the skaters ever so gracefully glide across the ice.

"This is lots of fun, sitting here with you and drinking hot chocolate, Miss James," she said, looking up into my eyes with a little lady smile.

I felt strange once again, as though she knew what I'd been thinking about her.

We finished our chocolate, tossed our paper cups in the tin garbage can next to the bench. I said, "Let's skate around the lake a bit longer. Then I have to get to the restaurant and begin painting my mural."

She smiled gaily, took my hand, and led me to the lakeside. "We won't ever skate together again. I want to remember today."

Instead of asking why we wouldn't skate again, I said, "Lulu, when did your sister Annie die?"

She looked toward the chocolate vendor building. Her eyes saddened. "Four years ago."

Then, without saying goodbye, she skated to the far end of the lake near where the orphanage used to be. She disappeared.

My ears popped.

14
Valentine's Day Invitation
Nyah

During the second week in February, early morning, at least it was early for me, Mary pounded on my door waking me up out of a deep sleep.

"Nyah, ya have a phone call," she said through the door.

"Okay. Be right there," I squeaked in my early morning scratchy voice.

I fumbled my way to the light switch and tripped on my slippers. I put on my pink bathrobe and new slippers and opened the door. A cold blast of winter wind swirled around my neck like a typhoon.

The telephone was at the end of the hallway outside Dave and Mary's apartment. She handed me the black receiver. I thanked her. I felt a brief drift of warmth coming from their apartment when Mary rushed back inside.

"Hello?" I squeaked.

The cheery voice of a woman said, "Good morning, Nyah. Did I wake you?"

I coughed a couple of times trying to clear my throat. "Who's this?"

"How quickly you forget, my dear. We had dinner a couple of weeks ago at the Sequim Bay Restaurant. Any clue yet?"

"Oh, shit! Hi Twiggy. I, well, I, ah . . ."

"Do you always stammer first thing out of bed?"

"I didn't think I'd ever hear from you again," was about all I could think of to say. I won't lie, I'd thought about Twiggy a lot.

"Your mural's showing progress. Suzie and Roger are excited about it. Listen, I know the Delmonico, and it can't be comfortable standing out in a cold hallway talking on the phone, so I'll get right to it. Will you have dinner with me Tuesday?"

"Ah, yeah, sure. Do you have anywhere special in mind?"

"I have a beach house on Discovery Bay. How about I pick you up after I get off work, say about seven? I'll cook us up a little something. Dress casually. Do you like champagne?"

"Seven would be great. I've never had champagne. Tuesday at seven, I'll be down in the bar talking to Dave. I'll keep an eye out for you. Drive up and park in front of the fire hydrant."

Telling me to dress casually was like telling me to dress up. She knew I wasn't a slave to fashion. I had starving artist stamped on my forehead in indelible red India ink.

"I hope you're not allergic to lobster."

"I've never had lobster," I answered. "What shall I bring?"

"Bring yourself. I'll pick you up the day after tomorrow in front of Dave's special parking spot."

I set the receiver back on the hook. Stupefied, I sat smiling and leaned back against Mary's door. Twiggy Carpenter had invited me to her beach house for dinner! I must have leaned too hard on Mary's door because when she opened it, I fell backward into her warm living room and landed on my hind-end.

"Whatcha doin'? Listening at ma door?"

I heard someone cough from across the room. "Oh, sorry. Hi, Dave. I didn't realize I was leaning on your door. Sorry." I gathered myself up from the floor.

I backed into the hallway, jetted to my room, shut the door behind me, and leaned against it in a daze. It occurred to me—Tuesday was February Fourteenth, Valentine's Day.

15
A Sexy Woman and My Lonesome Toothbrush
Nyah

The steam heater in my bathroom clanged and sputtered. Wearing my new pink bathrobe and matching slippers, which I'd bought from Penney's Department store, couldn't prevent my body from shivering. I found three candles in the cabinet beneath the sink and a box of Diamond Strike wooden matches and set them on the windowsill next to the tub. The match I struck sizzled, sending up a short burst of sulfur that plumed like feathers leaving a smell like rotten eggs. I filled the eagle claw tub almost to the brim, high enough so I could slowly sink beneath the water without an overflow. I tossed a cup of Epsom salts, a capful of rose water, and a good dose of Joy dishwashing liquid into the steaming water.

Nailed to the inside of the bathroom door was a four-foot-long mirror with a wood frame on which I'd nailed an old flour sack to prevent accidently seeing my face and body. To see myself stark naked could give nightmares. That evening I intrepidly removed the nails and let the flour sack fall to the floor.

I let my bathrobe slip off my shoulders and drop onto the hard-wood planks. My palm wiped away the steam on the mirror. Prickly sensations ran up my arms. I took in a quick breath. My breasts were smooth and lifted, my nipples pink and erect. My strawberry pubic hair pretty much matched the hair on my head, curly and shiny. My skinny arms hung down my side like noodles, and as for my toothpick legs, well, I hadn't shaved my legs since the first snowstorm of the winter. Until now I had no reason.

I slowly raised my gaze to my face. My peaches-and-cream skin and the speckled freckles near the edge of my Irish nose made me grin. I couldn't recall ever having looked into my eyes. I let my gaze peer deep into each of my pupils. My heart beat faster. Down my shoulders, shivers spread. I felt a sort of, well, self-love. My clear opal eyes were looking back at me, no longer bloodshot. I thought: Wow, I'm sort of pretty—sort of.

I kicked off my slippers and set them in front of my free-standing heater. I grabbed the new bar of Ivory soap from the crab-shaped soap dish. The light from the three candles flickered wavy shadows on the walls. I edged one toe into the bath. There I stood, one foot on the cold plank floor and the other inside the steaming spa. The sensation dazzled me. A deep breath extracted the steam from the tub and into my lungs. I slowly slipped my other foot into the tub and slid my prickling body into the hot water up to my neck and closed my eyes. My core slowly warmed, my scalp stopped quivering, my legs calmed, and I relaxed. The suds drifted me into a spell as the water enveloped me.

I floated into a sweet reverie with Twiggy Carpenter in the leading role. I imagined Twiggy lying naked next to me between blue flannel sheets. She kissed me and kissed me again. With my eyes closed I slowly let my knees separate. My back arched as the hot water rushed inside of me.

I held my nostrils shut and slid my head under the water. With sudsy water dripping into my eyes, I rubbed Prell shampoo into my hair until I had a full head of suds. I dunked my head again to rinse away most of the shampoo. I put a new steel razor blade into my Gillette Milady Decollete' shaver, soaped a good lather up each of my legs, and shaved from the top of my ankles to bottom of my knees. Then I shaved the stubble from under my arms. After each drag of my razor, I twisted the end of the shaver which opened the cover to the blade and rinsed the stubbles off under the faucet.

After my lavish bath, I popped the rubber plug and while the water was draining, I got down on hands and knees and twisted on the warm water faucet and rinsed my hair one last time. I stepped out of the tub onto a new Penney's bathmat and secured a towel around my wet hair with a clothespin, then wrapped myself in another bath towel and secured the closure with my last two clothespins. My slippers were warm and fluffy.

In the cracked mirror above the chipped white porcelain sink, I stared once again into my eyes. Seeing my rosy face brought a surge of feeling to my heart, sensations of excitement, eagerness, a sense of being a woman, a sexy woman. The slow scrutiny of my own features made me gasp, as though I were looking at a beautiful stranger living inside my skin. I dared to look past my opal blues into a deeper part of me, the part of me I'd never had the courage to view before I met Twiggy. I couldn't recall a time in my life I'd experienced a warm feeling about myself or being in love with my soul. I felt a powerful yearning of sexual ache, the desire a thirteen-year-old girl might feel when she first falls in love.

I leaned into the mirror and brushed my teeth with Bucky Beaver toothpaste, then dropped my lonesome toothbrush into the Mason jar next to the water faucet. I sprayed Stopette deodorant under my arms and applied makeup. Again, I stepped forward and scrutinized my features. My face was soft and smooth, my eyes framed in sable-colored Elizabeth Arden mascara and light blue eye shadow. I decided I didn't need rouge to brighten my cheeks, but I did smooth some peach-colored lipstick onto my winter dried lips. I'd saved my favorite task for last. I sprayed several spurts from my new bottle of Tabu cologne onto my shoulders, arms, and throat. The fragrant notes of rose, orange blossom, jasmine, and oak moss were so strong they made me cough. With a wet washrag, I scrubbed until my shoulders, arms, and throat were sore. I doubted the scent was gone, but I had no other perfume to wear.

Since I'd only bought one new outfit at the JC Penney store, I had no difficulty choosing which pair of cream-colored wool slacks or which navy-blue, cowl-neck, dolman-sleeved cashmere sweater to wear for my Valentine's date. I clipped on a pair of Penney's silver-plated earrings, the first earrings I'd ever had.

I liked my new haircut. I squeezed out a dab of mineral pomade into my palm and then into my hair which I combed up and back into the popular DA style. After my bright red fingernail polish dried, I found two shiny copper pennies and pressed them into the slots provided in my new penny loafers. I put on my new full-length brown duster jacket and dashed downstairs to the bar to await Twiggy's arrival. Somehow, being dressed up unlocked all my emotions. I felt pretty, and I felt happy, and so afraid!

16
Tabu
Nyah

Twiggy was on time picking me up for our date. As I stood at the front window of the One-Eyed Dog, she eased her coupe to the curb in front of the fire hydrant. When I stepped into her Bullet-Nose, the scent of Chanel Number Five swirled around my head and set my heart ablaze. She wore a chic tweed suit over a mauve-colored cashmere sweater along with a short string of pearls and mauve-colored suede penny loafers.

"You look great, Nyah! What a beauty," Twiggy said, after I shut the car door.

"Really? I only wear this outfit when I don't care how I look," I teased. "Actually, I dropped into the JC Penney's on Water Street to get something new to wear."

"Funny girl. And I love your new hairdo." She glanced into her side mirror and drove on.

"Yeah, I also stopped in the beauty shop next door to Penney's. I asked for a ducktail cut, but my DA looks more like an HA."

"An HA?"

"A horse's ass."

"It does not, Nyah." Twiggy chuckled. "You look lovely, including your hair. Are you wearing Tabu?"

"Twiggy, you've been working all day and not one hair on your head is out of place," I said, changing the subject. I was appalled she could still smell the pungent odor, even after my struggle to scrub it off. "How is it Dave can park his coupe in front of the fire hydrant?"

She smiled. "I guess because he plays poker with the police chief."

"So, what do you do as a reporter?"

"Last week I covered a story over in Port Hadlock outside of town. An entire family lost their lives."

"What happened?"

"During this winter storm many families are without heat."

"No, please don't tell me."

"They used one of those small portable barbecues to burn Presto logs and green wood inside the house. They went to bed with the fire still smoldering and were asphyxiated. The three kids, including a one-year-old and an old dog, all found dead by neighbors the next morning. The parents meant well, but they were ignorant about the dangers."

"Oh, my dear God."

"I spend time in court reporting on cases of public interest. I know the judge, prosecutor, and police by first name. Every once in a while, they call me or stop by my house to give me a heads up about anything newsworthy going on."

"I'm sure a woman such as yourself has some fun hobbies to help take your spirit out of the criminal world," I probed.

Twiggy was silent.

After a short trip out of town, Twiggy coasted her Bullet-Nose down a short road and slid into a long and curvy driveway, which brought us up to the back door of her white two-story Victorian beach house.

"Wow."

"Wow, what?"

"This is your beach house?"

Twiggy laughed. "What did you think I meant when I said I have a beach house?"

"I was thinking beach—cabin."

"Nope, funny girl. I hope your expectations aren't disappointed. Come on, let's go inside."

I was pleasantly surprised to find the premises cozy and warm. Twiggy drooped our coats across a bench inside the back porch.

"Wow," I repeated.

"Nyah, you make me laugh. What are you wowing about? Come, I'll give you a tour."

We walked down the hallway past the laundry room and into the kitchen.

I gasped. "You must have every modern tool and appliance known to humans. I've never seen a pink kitchen before, not to mention turquoise appliances. Oh, what beautiful red roses!"

"Read the card."

I opened the tiny envelope and pulled out the card: *For Nyah, from your friend, Twiggy.*

"Twiggy, I don't know what to say. They're beautiful." Feeling shy and my face warming, I glanced quickly into her soft celestial eyes. She smiled. A tiny butterfly fluttered its wings inside my bosom. My lips parted. I had a desire to kiss her.

"Here, a small offering of my friendship to you." Twiggy handed me a small box wrapped in white tissue paper and a pink shiny ribbon.

Like a kid at Christmas, I greedily slipped off the ribbon and tore off the wrapping paper. Inside was a bottle of Chanel Number Twenty-Two perfume. "Thank you, Twiggy. I didn't know Chanel made Number Twenty-Two." I dabbed some behind my left ear.

Twiggy tickled her nose in the crook of my neck. "Yum, the scent of Number Twenty-Two is luscious on you." When her nose touched my neck, goosebumps spread across my back from shoulder to shoulder.

"I thought I heard you come home, Miss Carpenter," a middle-aged Asian woman said, as she walked into the kitchen. "Your dinner ingredients are in the refrigerator." She smiled at me and seemed to take no notice of Twiggy's arm wrapped around my waist.

"Kissoon, this is my friend, Nyah, Nyah James. She's on her way to being a very well-known artist. Nyah, please meet my housekeeper, Kissoon Choo."

We shook hands. She said, "Have a nice time tonight you two. I'm going home to feed my husband."

Kissoon Choo cuddled into her long winter coat and closed the back door behind her.

"Let's finish our tour." Twiggy took my hand as we stepped into her magnificent combination living room and formal dining area.

I marveled, "I've never seen such high ceilings in a house before. Of course, I've never been in a house like this."

"Fifteen feet high—Douglas fir from the local lumber mill. The white oak floor planks are from the mill, too."

I looked out the tinted windows overlooking the expanse of Discovery Bay, the sky filled with ever-blinking stars; the waning crescent moon shimmered over the bay. I wondered what her view of the bay would be like on a spring morning.

Several enormous oriental rugs covered the floor in each of the rooms. There were two overstuffed cream-colored davenports and chairs, a black mahogany dining table and dining chairs, and a six-foot wet bar facing the bay. I was totally overwhelmed while trying to take it all in. Especially beautiful was a beige carpeted, fifteen-foot-wide white spiral stairway with black wooden handrails corkscrewing up the stairs.

"Come sit at the bar. I'll be back with our champagne."

Moments later, she arrived carrying a sterling silver tray with two crystal champagne flutes bubbling with champagne and one of my red roses in a stemmed crystal vase. She placed the tray on the white marble bar.

"I'll be back with the prawn cocktails."

"Twiggy, what a pretty plate," I said, when she reentered the dining room.

Twiggy squirted some freshly sliced tart lemon on top of cooled pink prawns on a bed of head lettuce. I jumped a little and pretended to wipe away lemon juice from my eye. "I've never had prawn cocktails before."

"Did I squirt lemon juice in your eye? Sorry!"

"No, just kidding."

"You do make me laugh, Nyah."

In the middle of the plate was a small dish containing a red sauce and two quarters of lemon. My mouth watered anticipating biting into the lemons.

"You've never had prawn cocktails?" Twiggy asked, as she slowly leaned over and kissed me, dancing her tongue with mine. "You taste wonderful, Nyah."

My face warmed. The hair on my arms stood up like little peach-colored flags. I never in a thousand years thought Twiggy would be attracted to me any more than as a friend. Shivers waved up my spine.

Without making a big deal about kissing me, she picked up a tiny fork and stabbed a piece of red prawn and dipped it in the red sauce. "Open wide."

I opened wide, and she inserted the tiny fork between my lips.

"Now close your lips and bite down." She slid the fork from my mouth.

I closed my lips and bit down. The tartness of the lemon reacted with the glands under my tongue; my entire face grimaced like a little kid biting into a dill pickle.

"So? Do you like prawn cocktails?" Twiggy teased.

"Ambrosia," I responded, my mouth still puckered.

"Not so much, huh?"

"No, really, I like it when my face scrunches into a scary mask."

"You're so funny, Nyah. The melting snow's agreeing with you."

"No, I'm tiring of the snow. Not having a driver's license or a vehicle to get around in has been a major barrier for me."

"You don't have a driver's license?" Twiggy asked. "Have you ever had a license?"

"No. But don't tell Dave."

"Why not?"

"I'm borrowing his car this weekend to drive to the gallery. I have another set of drawings."

"Oh, I see. Say, if you study for the driver's test and pass it, I have a cherried-out 1948 baby-blue Starlight Studebaker coupe I could sell you. In the meantime, I'll drive you to the gallery."

"I'm pretty sure I wouldn't have the money to buy a fancy car like a Starlight."

"It's just sitting in my garage since I bought my new Bullet-Nose. It has a four-panel, wrap-around back window. Very chic. If three hundred dollars is more than you have right now, you may pay me in installments. It has whitewall tires, of course."

"Twiggy, what a dream come true for me, but—"

"No buts about it. I consider my baby-blue baby all yours." Twiggy pressed her warm cheek to mine and pulled back, raising her champagne flute. "Here's to your career as an artist, and to our new friendship. Oh, and happy Valentine's Day."

My crotch was throbbing.

We locked our elbows together and clicked our champagne flutes, and sipped champagne. Twiggy smiled, looked into my eyes, slowly moved her head toward me, caressed my cheeks with her long fingers, and gently pressed her lips on my mouth and kissed me again. The heat of her lips melting on mine sent shockwaves through my belly. Another kiss. She parted my lips with hers and caressed my tongue. Her wet mouth opened my heart, relaxed me, and caused my sweet warm wetness to flow.

"I care about you, Nyah," she whispered. "You're a beautiful lady, and you make me laugh."

"Twiggy, I'm overwhelmed. I've warm feelings for you, too."

Avoiding her eyes, I glanced around the music room. I gasped. "Wow, a piano."

She wrapped her arm around my waist as we strolled to her piano room. I felt the warmth of her skin through my sweater.

"A Steinway Chippendale," I noted, reading the label above the keyboards.

"Solid brass pedals and wheels, ebonized mahogany," Twiggy said.

"I dare not even touch this beautiful work of art." I pressed the palm of my hand to my heart.

"You have tears in your eyes. Here, sit down."

I didn't sit down; I wanted her to keep her arm around my waist.

Near her Steinway, two rows, each of six high-back chairs, stood at attention like soldiers, in the same color and texture as her piano. I guessed they were Chippendale. "You have your own concert hall?"

"Please, have a seat." Twiggy pointed and I sat in the front row.

"I gather people come to listen to you play."

"I play a little." Her smile warmed my thighs.

Twiggy sat on her piano bench, posed her feet over the soft and sustain pedals, studied the keyboard, and began striking the keys with energy. The entire room radiated pure musical notes, octaves echoing around the room, reflecting off the walls and ceiling, her house miraculously coming alive. Each note had a voice of its own and resonated deeply within my soul. The experience took my breath away.

She tickled the ivory and black keys to the tune of "The Boogie Woogie Bugle Boy of Company B," a popular song by the Andrews Sisters. I again witnessed Twiggy's soft light blue-green aura glowing around her head. Why is she so mindful of me? I puzzled. After the last chords echoed into silence, she got up and took my hand and escorted me to the dining room.

"Twiggy, seriously, do you play professionally? I've never heard music played with such passion and clarity." My thoughts focused on the heat from her kiss which had sent a lightning bolt to my navel.

"I've played, yes. Granny, my mum's mother, was a concert pianist in her time. I started playing the piano when I was four. Granny tutored me and guided me every step of the way. Mum made it clear music was a hobby for women, and journalism was important and had merit. It's time for dinner, my dear."

"Concert pianist? Is this the topic you didn't want to talk about the other night?"

"Yeah, it's what I meant when I told Suzie how tired I get when I'm on tour for weeks at a time. Music's in my blood—always has been. We only have so much time here on earth, so I went out into the world and made my passion for music happen.

"Mum's a powerful woman. Going against her wishes to focus on journalism was unbearable, but necessary. Granny always told us kids,

'If you don't make something of your life, who will?' Nyah, you may not know it, but somewhere deep inside your soul, you've known this truth as well. You knew what you wanted to do, and you set out and did it, and it's paying off for you. I'm proud of your stamina."

As we walked arm-in-arm back to the kitchen, shelves of record albums came into view. "Wow, am I to presume you also collect record albums?"

"Music's my passion. For my seventh birthday, Granny bought me this phonograph and my first seventy-eight-rpm record. The 1920s was the decade of the Roaring Twenties, the Jazz Age."

"What record did Granny buy?"

Twiggy reached to the top shelf and picked out a record album. "It's Duke Ellington's 'Black and Tan Fantasy.' It's a beautiful rendition of the unsettled state of the human soul. The growling trumpet, dissonant piano interludes, muted, wailing trombone ruminations. Then it concludes with a musical rendition from Chopin's 'Funeral March.'"

"Your granny sounds like she was a thoughtful woman."

"She's still my main source of love and support," Twiggy said, setting the record next to the phonograph.

"She's still with us?"

"Yep, and I love her with all my heart. Would you like to listen to it?"

"Of course, I'd love to."

Twiggy slipped the record from its sleeve, then gently placed her hands on each side and set it on the felt mat, then cranked the handle a few times. She rotated the swing arm onto the record and flipped up the brake release switch. Once the music began, she rotated the volume button.

After the music stopped, she slid the record back into the sleeve and stood on her toes to replace it on the top shelf.

Awed, I said, "That was a beautiful recording. I have goosebumps up and down my arms. How many records do you have in your collection?"

"One thousand thirty-two. Are you getting hungry? Oh, by the by, have you ever had lobster bisque?"

17
One Girl Survived; Her Friend Suffocated
Nyah

"Lobster *what*?"

"Ha, ha, well, we're going to make it together. It'll be fun." Twiggy smiled as we sashayed hand in hand into the expanse of her kitchen. Hand in hand!

Kissoon had the kitchen pots and pans ready for us to make our dinner. Twiggy grabbed two huge living lobsters from a ten-gallon pot. Kissoon had started boiling the water prior to going home.

"What're we going to do with living lobsters?" I asked, flooding into shock.

"Dunk the heads into the boiling water and quickly let go." She dropped the lobsters back into the ten-gallon pot. "What do you think, funny girl? Now, reach into the pot from behind the claws, grab it, hold it tightly. Here, I'll show you."

She picked out two aprons from a lower drawer and tied mine behind mine back. As hard as I tried to put my hand into the pot and grab a live lobster, I couldn't do it. Needless to say, Twiggy expertly grabbed both lobsters and dropped them head-first and one at a time into the pot of boiling water. Upon hitting the hot water, the lobsters actually screamed.

Once lobsters were dead, they turned red. We cut them in half lengthwise, hacked off the tails, claws, and knuckles with cooking shears, and cut them into two-inch pieces, shell and all. In a stockpot we heated three tablespoons of oil, one tablespoon of garlic, three diced shallots, one large, chopped onion, four peeled carrots, five celery stalks, a small can of tomato paste, and finally, all the lobster claws and tail pieces. We cooked it all for ten minutes. Then we used a clasping tool and lifted them out of the pan and set them aside.

"Now we'll deglaze the pan with sherry."

"Deglaze?"

"Here, let me show you." Twiggy poured white wine into the hot stockpot. Using a whisk, she quickly whipped the liquid, scraping loose the browned garlic, onion and lobster bits and pieces off the bottom of the pot. "Now we'll add one tablespoon of whole black pepper corns, fresh thyme leaves, and small can of tomato puree. Take the wooden spoon and stir it for five minutes."

She added a quart of water and a quart of heavy whipping cream and brought the mixture to a boil. "It's time to take the lobster meat out of the shells and set them on the butcher block in the green bowl. But don't toss the shells, we're going to put them in the stock and simmer until the stock reduces about twenty-five percent."

"Reduces?"

Twiggy put another pot on the stove and melted half a cup of butter and stirred in a half a cup of flour with a wire whisk until the roux was blond in color. "Okay Nyah. The stock is reduced. Hold this colander over the roux pan and I'll pour this mixture into the colander. Be careful. I don't want you burned." Once the mixture was strained, I tossed the shells and veggie mixture into the trash.

"Will you whisk the mixture for me?" asked Twiggy. "I'll chop the lobster meat into half inch pieces, and you whisk them together into the bisque. Oh, we forgot to chop a quarter cup of chives for garnish. Go ahead and chop them and also a half cup of parsley. I'll add one eighth teaspoon of cayenne, a half cup of cream sherry, and we'll add salt and fresh ground black pepper to taste."

"Wow. The kitchen smells delicious!" I said, while I chopped chives and parsley.

"All right now, let's get to eating!" Twiggy grasped the two handles of the soup tureen. "I'm hungry," she added.

I held open one of the swinging kitchen doors. Twiggy, like the sophisticate she was, pranced through the doors like Lana Turner and placed the soup tureen at the end of the long dining table where we were to be seated next to each other. The shiny, dark wood table was about eight feet long and set for two. She'd placed a long narrow cloth down the middle of the table and placed my red rose flower vase in the center, and finally, dinnerware with a gray bamboo art pattern.

"I'll get the salad, be right back." Returning to the dining room, she said, "I'll do the honors," and dipped the ladle into the tureen to portion out our lobster bisque into the ceramic bowls, and we garnished it with the chopped chives and a pinch of onion.

I said, "Once I find a house with a kitchen, I'll be able to cook for you, but for now, Mary at the One-Eye is my chef."

"You'll cook for me?" Twiggy asked. "Promise?"

"I'll have to learn how to cook first. But I learn fast." I felt my face burn.

"Let's eat." Twiggy leaned down to smell the hot steam wafting off her bowl. "Smells wonderful."

I slurped a spoonful of the creamy bisque, and the taste exploded in my mouth. After a moment of savoring the essence of our creation, I said, "Twiggy, this is delicious!"

"It is sweet and succulent."

"I love the butter and white wine taste."

"The lobster tastes like a cross between crab and shrimp. So, I've been meaning to ask you. Did you ever find out more about the little girl in the park?"

Stunned, I asked, "How do you know about the little girl in the park?"

"I dropped by the Cape Flattery Art Gallery a few days ago. I also cover the art scene and new artists for the *Gazette*. Frank and Kayte showed me your pen and ink drawings. They told me you noticed her in a park."

"It's so odd. Last month, I was slogging through the uptown park with my portfolio under my arm trying to find my way back downtown. The snow was freezing my face and the wind pushed me and I fell backward. When I was finally able to stand, my ears popped. In an instant, the park went quiet and the storm stopped, and I saw a tiny shadow, a figure, sitting on one of the park benches. She was alone and wearing a flour bag for a dress. No coat, no hat, no stockings. She was talking to a ragdoll."

Twiggy looked up from her bisque and stared at me. "Your ears popped?" she asked. "Interesting. Why was she sitting there in the cold?"

"I have no idea why. She said she lived at the orphanage around the lake. Of course, I took her hand and walked her to the orphanage."

"Orphanage?" Twiggy asked. "The town orphanage was torn down around 1890, and a Victorian house was built on the site a few years later. Have you seen her since the park?"

"Yes. About a week later I ran into her while skating on the lake."

"Did your ears pop then?"

"Yeah, they did. What are you implying?" I asked. Her question gave me a creepy sensation.

"I'm not sure why I asked that. This whole story sounds a bit macabre. Did you have contact with her at the lake?"

"Yeah. I'd only been skating a minute or so when she skated up to me with a big smile on her face. She was two feet taller than she was when I saw her in the park. She said she was nine years old and that her sister died from suffocation from breathing black dust. She took my hand and pulled me around on the ice."

"These sightings are very odd."

"While we skated, I asked her when her sister died, and she said four years ago. But when we met in the park, she said her sister was sick in present time, not four years ago. She's an enigma for sure."

I took another sparkling sip of champagne and gently dabbed the corner of my mouth with my napkin and placed the napkin back on my lap without it falling on the floor. Twiggy was running her toe up my calf. A tingling sensation wiggled down my thigh.

"Thank God I'm in the possession of her doll, or I might be questioning my sanity."

"It sounds like she was talking like a Dust Bowl survivor. You say you're in possession of this doll?"

"Yep, I have it back in my room. She talked about the Great Depression and the Dust Bowl of the 1930s. Wait a moment. Did you say the orphanage was torn down in the early 1890s?"

"Yes. A fire started in the kitchen. The children on the main floor and in the kitchen burned to death. Two of the four Catholic nuns survived. The remaining nuns reported that two of the girls—close friends—were in the attic. Only one of those girls survived; her friend suffocated. The building was later condemned and torn down."

Twiggy slowly sipped another spoonful of bisque. The tingling in my thigh was more intense.

"But I helped her up the stairs to the orphanage door the night I met her," I protested. "When she disappeared, I looked through the window and the place was pitch black and empty. There's something so very odd about her. When I was with her, I felt like I was in a dream, but not in a dream."

"I'll talk to Mum about it. She's the expert on the Dust Bowl."

We finished dinner. I looked over Twiggy's shoulder, into her piano room. I noticed frames on the wall behind the chairs. "Would you mind showing me your hangings in your piano room?"

"Sure. Let's bring our champagne with us."

"Wow," I said moments later. "Is that you standing next to President Roosevelt in the Oval office? And here's another photo of you and President Truman! Who are you, seriously? Wow, both presidents signed the photos."

"And I signed both of the presidents' copies of their photos, too. I guess I'm sort of a renowned concert pianist in my spare time." She stood on one foot with her other heel leaning against her naked ankle, smiling at her images.

"You played private concerts for two presidents in the White House! Wait a moment, I saw you and a lady dancing the other night at the Hullabaloo. The next day I asked Dave who you were, and he said your name is Twiggy. That's how I recognized you during dinner that night."

"But enough about me. Kissoon made crème brûlée."

"I'll refresh our champagne."

Returning to the dining room, Twiggy pushed open the swinging kitchen door with her shapely derriere. "Crème brûlée served, my friend." She set the desserts on our lace dinner mats. The scent of vanilla and caramel wafted under my nose as it passed by.

"Have you ever eaten crème brûlée?"

"No, and I'm embarrassed you asked," I said, feeling out of my social element.

"You're in for a new adventure," Twiggy teased. "It's an art in itself. "Watch the crème brûlée queen in action."

With the edge of her spoon she cracked the caramelized surface, shattering it like a windshield. I copied her. Then she used the tip of her spoon and loosened the crunchy edges from the ramekin. I copied her. Together we savored the buttery delight.

After we finished with our desserts, Twiggy scooted her chair from the table and without breaking eye contact, walked to me with her hand outreached. Our fingertips touched. She moved in close, released my fingers. With gentle precision, she softly stroked my cheek. Her hair held the scent of Prell shampoo. When her lips brushed against my own, I wrapped my arms around her shoulders and opened my mouth, fully receiving her soft, warm tongue. Her kiss was caramelized vanilla. She moved her mouth to my ear. Her warm breath blowing in my ear sent shivers across my shoulders.

My loins were a burning bush. I pulled my sweater up over my head and took off my sweater. Twiggy unsnapped my bra and cupped my breasts in her hands. And ever so gently, she suckled my nipples, first one then the other. Then she unzipped my slacks which fell down to my ankles.

"Let's lie down on the carpet, Nyah," Twiggy said, her respiration heavy and fast.

Twiggy slipped off my loafers and helped me out of my slacks. We lay on the carpet, Twiggy at my side caressing my breasts and stroking my belly. My heart was racing in anticipation. I guided her hand until I felt her fingers in my vagina.

"Relax, honey. Let the sweetness happen."

I let it happen.

We fell asleep near the heat of the fireplace in each other's arms. We woke up in the dark. Hand in hand we walked up the stairs and fell asleep in Twiggy's bed.

► ■ ◄

The next morning, after cinnamon toast and coffee, Twiggy and I entered her garage where she showed me her Studebaker Starlight.

"Here she is. She's waiting for you. She's road and snow ready. But this morning I'm driving you back to the hotel. I'm making sure my darling Nyah gets back to her apartment safely."

Twiggy put her Bullet-Nose into the parked position letting the engine idle. She leaned over to me and gently caressed my cheeks in her hands and kissed me lightly, warmly, and with passion. And I kissed her back. The wetness of her kiss sent shivers to my thighs.

She dropped me off at the Delmonico in front of the fire hydrant. "Drive with care," I said, stepping onto the sidewalk. I shut the door. From the rearview mirror, I saw her throw me a kiss.

18
Like A Dead Crow
Nyah

At midnight, an evil force snatched my six-year-old soul. It dragged me high above Thunder Edge. The Strait of Juan de Fuca whizzed by beneath me. The gigantic, creaking weeping willows near the edge of the precipice were swiftly dwarfed and uprooted by the wrath of the wind, and the cliff lurched, winding along its path. As the streak of the rocky abyss spun into a mere thread, it sprawled into land. The long bony finger of the bluff pointed west, and the evil forced me to my destination. Musty gusts sucked breath from my tortured lungs. My paralyzed body hurled first west to the open Pacific Ocean, and south again following the void.

Inky streaks of clouds, giant strokes of a madman's brush, randomly smeared the face of the man on the moon and stained the angry sea. Overgrown blackberry bushes squeezed thorny arms around rain-soaked telephone poles in a queer embrace. Thick black moss encroached upon the concrete and mingled with overgrown yellow heads of dandelion. The arms of blackberry bushes reached out, grabbed me, and tore my dangling feet.

In an instant I fell from the midnight sky like a dead crow. The blasting winds of the fall pierced through my ears and yanked my curly hair straight up as the earth's gravity sucked me down into the dark chasm. The leaf-bare branches of weeping willow trees grabbed onto each other in a strong embrace just in time to catch my limp body and set me down inches above the wet grasses.

Stark-raving terror forced open my eyes. I was sitting on the soaked ground surrounded by ruins of gravestones. Gray human bones, jagged shards, were strewn everywhere. Black clouds dumped rain, drenching my trembling body. Deafening thunder rattled the ground beneath my useless legs. Another, and again another. Blinding bolts of white lightning stabbed my eyes.

I strained to run, but I was a ragdoll. I tried to scream through lungs devoid of air. I had no sense of cold, but my arms shivered as they fell limp at my side. My keen sense of smell overwhelmed me. The sour stench of yesterday, the stinking sweat of an old man, penetrated my burning nostrils. Lightning bolts stabbed deep into the unhallowed grounds. Tombstones blasted into pieces and flung high into the sky. Blasting thunder impaling the souls of the dead.

He stood in front of me. My ears rang from his voice and the grinning whisper of him. His blood-veined eyes forced me to follow him. Trapped, I gave up the struggle. I floated behind him. He stood behind a rotting rain-stained wooden ladder teetering against the decrepit woodshed. His sweat-stained bib overalls sported faded blue stripes, with a large tear at the right knee. His dank odor permeated my nostrils. He wore no shirt. His mud brown hat, sweat stains around the band, drooped down over his forehead. Gray spider fingers reached out as he stepped backwards into the doorway. Terror choked me. All of a sudden, I was inside the dank woodshed. The heavy door slammed shut behind me. He stank like a drunken dead coyote. The mighty wind tore off my clothes. He shoved me up the ladder and pushed me down onto the pile of straw. I fought him, kicked him. He pressed me down. His sharp fingernails were inside my vagina. In a moment my soul snapped loose and hovered above him in the corner of the ceiling. From above I watched what he was doing. He pulled my legs apart. I screamed, but the words were absorbed by mounds of haystacks.

I heard a thud. My soul snapped back in my tiny body. His hat flew off his head; he fell heavily upon my belly. He stopped moving.

Someone, whose face I didn't see, someone whose voice I knew not, slammed a short piece of wood against the wall. The person shoved him on his back. The blow from the piece of wood split his head open. Blood oozed and carved streams down his neck, soaking into the hay.

His right ear hung, attached only by a long piece of gray skin. His eyes twitched and became red copper pennies.

My savior wore a red rain cape with an attached hood, and hundreds of honeybees cloaked her like a jacket. I heard the woman say gently, "Don't be frightened, Ladybug. The honeybees won't harm you."

I woke from the nightmare. My heart pounded against my ribs. Sitting on my chair, next to my bed, was the little girl whose name was Lulu. She was wearing a clean, sleeveless dress sewn out of white flour sacks with red crocheted rosebuds sewn into the fabric, holding her ragdoll in her lap. I blinked and the child vanished into a lilac-colored mist, leaving the ragdoll leaning against the back of my chair.

19
The Dust Bowl Era
Nyah

At noon, Twiggy picked me up at the Delmonico and we drove to Discovery Bay to meet her mother, who, she said, would be interested in my mysterious Lulu sightings. Similar to Twiggy's driveway—long and curvy—her mother's driveway was finished with graveled stone which ended at a detached two-car garage. As we approached the top of the driveway, into view came a modest two-story Victorian home perched on a hill, with a high-bank view of Discovery Bay.

The house was white with turquoise-trimmed window shutters. And the double front doors were turquoise with opaque twinkling windows at the top. The indigo winter sky framed the house and shake roof, and the Olympic Mountain peaks jutted behind the vast wildfire fields on the other side of a creek. Peeking over the hill was a beautiful lavender field, and on the other side of the house was a wooded area of white birch trees. The white bark of the trees was peeling off in long strips, and the branches were beginning the annual sprouting of long catkins. We parked in the driveway.

With playful guidance, holding my hand, Twiggy navigated us around to the front door facing the bay. After several quick rings of the doorbell, in we strolled.

"Hello, we're here!" Twiggy called. We took our shoes off and moved toward the huge expanse of her mother's kitchen. Someone was playing a piano.

From around the corner a cheerful, striking lady bounded over to greet us with her hands outstretched. Her beauty was timeless. I guessed her to be in her sixties. Her short titanium hair with curly bangs highlighted her black round eyeglasses which slid down over the end of her straight nose. Twiggy certainly had inherited this woman's imperial blue eyes.

"Granny," Twiggy said, in a sweet voice. They kissed each other on the lips. "I didn't know you'd be here, Gran, but I'm happy you are. I'd like you to meet my good friend, Nyah James. Nyah, this is my mother's mother, my grandma, Twiggy Carpenter, Senior."

"Hello Mrs. Carpenter. Nice to meet you." I shook her warm hand, but she wrapped her arms around me and gave me a jiggly, snuggly hug.

"Please call me Twiggy, dear," she said, with a smile.

Right behind Twiggy's grandma, another woman entered the room from the swinging kitchen door. Twiggy scurried over and kissed her on her cheek. The woman didn't kiss her back.

"Mummy, I'd like you to meet my friend, Nyah James, Nyah, this is my mum, Twiggy Carpenter, Junior."

Her mother and grandma looked very much like twins, though her mother was not wearing glasses and was much younger.

"Wow," I said, shaking her hand. Her mother was aloof. Her handshake was loose, and she dropped her limp, ice-cold hand from mine quickly. Her gaze was cool, distant.

"Nice to meet you," I offered. "What should I call you?"

"Twiggy," she answered, flatly.

The magical notes of musical octaves were resonating from the back of the house. Granny—Twiggy Senior—headed across the living area, peeked around the corner, and called, "Claudia, our company's here."

The piano playing stopped, but the magical notes continued vibrating into space.

Around the corner, Granny and another striking woman bounded over to us, hand in hand, wearing wide grins.

"Claudia," Granny said, "meet Miss Nyah James, Twiggy's artist friend. Nyah, with pleasure I introduce you to my life partner, Claudia."

"We've been together since we were thirty," Claudia said. "We met in graduate school. But we grew up in the same neighborhood in the uptown area."

"She's put up with me for fifty-five years and counting." Granny chuckled. Granny and Claudia kissed each other on the lips.

"Yeah, can you believe I've spent fifty-five years with this woman?" Claudia said, as she gazed into her love's eyes. "What I mean is, time has no meaning living my life with her. Come. Let's relax at the kitchen table."

"Nyah, would you like a glass of wine, a Coca-Cola?" Granny asked.

"Sure, I'd love a Coke, with ice. Thanks."

"Say, Nyah," Claudia said, "Granny has a painting of yours hanging in her office at the paper. It's your interpretation of the Strait of Juan de Fuca. Twiggy, your Twiggy, has had her eye on it, wanting it for herself."

"I couldn't believe it when she said you had a painting of mine." We sat at the informal kitchen table. "Back to what you were saying before, about time having no meaning. It's what the little girl who called herself Lulu told me. Has Twiggy mentioned the little girl I met in the park?"

Twiggy's granny and Claudia shared a quick glance.

"Excuse me," Twiggy's mother said, abruptly. "I'll be right back." A few minutes later she brought the two drawings I'd sketched of Lulu.

I stuttered, "Where—I mean, wow."

"Kayte and I are friends. She loaned me your art."

"Not to mention Kayte's my little sister," Claudia said, smiling.

"But I didn't tell her why I wanted them," Twiggy's mother said. "I think she believes I want to display them in my home."

"You and Miss Kayte are sisters, Claudia?" I asked. "There's the explanation for why you both have sterling silver eyes. I've never seen gray eyes before."

Twiggy's mother set the drawings on a couple of easels situated on the table. All three ladies stepped back for a better view.

"What is it you want to find out about this girl?" Twiggy's granny asked.

"We don't know where she lives," Twiggy said, in answer for me. "We know nothing other than she said her sister died from suffocation brought on by black dust, as the girl called it."

"She told me she wants to be a traveler and study history. The girl said the nuns were teaching that Hitler is the Chancellor of Germany." Again, Granny and Claudia gave each other a glance.

"Look at the dramatic way she ages in a week, from the first time you met her in the park to the following week when you went skating with her," Twiggy's mother said, gesturing at the pictures. "Nyah, you're certain you've touched her and talked to her?"

"Oh, I'm certain, all right." Her question caused my face to flush. "These are paintings of the girl who calls herself Lulu. I felt her hand in my hand. I still have the ragdoll in my room, the ragdoll she left behind in the park."

"You say her name was Lulu?" Granny asked.

"That's what she said," I answered, noticing Granny and Claudia looking at each other, the kind of look two people exchange when they know something others don't.

"I found some newspaper photos of the orphanage in various stages of demolition." Twiggy's mother spread the old newspaper images on the kitchen table. "Here's a few of the fire that destroyed most of the building in 1891. And here's more during the time of dismantling, and still more when they were tearing it down."

"The stained-glass door in this photo is the same stained-glass design I noticed the night I stood at the door to the orphanage," I said.

"You say you helped the girl to the front door of the orphanage?" Twiggy's mother asked, incredulously.

"I walked her right up to the gray stone steps. These photos look exactly like the orphanage I saw. I bent down and picked up her ragdoll she left behind, but she'd already vanished."

"After the orphanage burned down in 1891, the city demolished it," Granny said. "A Victorian house was built on the site in 1905.

Only one family has lived in the house, a father, mother, three children, and a dog called Cleo. And oh, yes, two black crows and an owl. A year later, the family packed up their Ford station wagon and flew the coop. It's been vacant over forty years."

Again, Granny and Claudia exchanged a knowing glance, raising my discomfort level.

"And the dog they called Cleo was left behind," Claudia said. "Local lore has it the dog went looney; it barked all night long for a year."

"What ever happened to the poor dog?" I asked.

All the Twiggys and Claudia gawked at each other.

"As the story goes, it jumped off the bluff," Claudia said. "Its body was broken in half. Poor thing."

"But why would a house remain vacant for over forty years?" I asked.

"The fire started in the middle of the night," Granny said, changing the subject. "Most of the children perished. All but two nuns who taught at the orphanage also perished. The crows, and the owl stayed."

"The house is haunted," Claudia said. "Are you superstitious, Nyah?"

"Let's put it this way, I have a healthy respect for the spirit world. Actually, I've been thinking about looking for a house to buy here in town. The crows stayed?"

"Yep, and the owl," answered Twiggy's grandma with a grin.

"Really? You're looking for a house?" asked Twiggy's mother.

"If I don't buy a house now, while I'm selling my work, when will I ever get another chance?"

"I'll call my realtor friend in the morning," Twiggy's mother said. "Trust me when I tell you she'll sell the place at a very low cost, very low. If you're serious and put down a pittance of cash, you could likely move in right away, rent free for six months or more, I have no doubt. If you fall in love with the place, if no ghosts of yesteryear haunt you right out of there, six months should give you time to clean and paint the place to your own specifications."

"What? Wow. You can't be serious."

"Let's take a look at it tomorrow, Nyah," Twiggy said. "Oh, Nyah brought the ragdoll with us. It's in my car. Be right back."

A few moments later, Twiggy, shivering from the cold air, ambled into the kitchen with the ragdoll in hand.

Twiggy's family examined the doll.

"I know for a fact this ragdoll was created in 1915, it's an original," Twiggy's granny said. "And yet it looks and feels spanking new."

"This means this doll is over thirty-five years old," Twiggy's mother said.

I said, "To me, Lulu looked to be five, maybe six, the first time I met her. The math doesn't work, does it?"

Claudia examined the doll. "For the girl to be say age five or six, she would have to be born about 1944, which would mean when she received the doll it must have been a hand-me-down. And yet the clothes on this doll are clean and wrinkle-free as though she'd taken it out of the box it came in."

"If she was born in 1944, it would have been as the Dust Bowl years were coming to an end," Twiggy's mom said. "So, it is possible her story about her sister dying from the Oklahoma black dust might be true."

Twiggy said, "Let's remember, though, the girl appeared to Nyah a week or so after their meeting in the park, and she looks like she was about nine in this drawing. So, it's a moot point talking about the year she was born. The girl's aging, and fast."

"The Dust Bowl wasn't a natural catastrophe, as most people tend to believe," Twiggy's mother said, looking out the huge bay window. "The Dirty Thirties were a human disaster, literally of biblical pro-portions."

Claudia said, "When the Homestead Act expanded, over thirty-two-thousand immigrants settled on public land. They plowed up the land over and over again until the fields turned into a sandy loam."

"When the stock market crashed in twenty-nine, no one could afford to buy the wheat," Twiggy's mother said. "In two years, thirty million acres of the Oklahoma grasslands were stripped of sod."

Granny took up the narrative. "Coyotes were killing livestock. And farmers were clubbing coyotes and jackrabbits by the tens of thousands."

"Having firsthand experience as a journalist," Twiggy's mother said, "when the wind and sand blew, the pain was like butcher knives cutting into your flesh, tearing through your bare legs, your face, and arms. Chickens, horses, and cattle lost their way and perished."

Claudia said, "One day a little five-year-old girl was outside playing when a black blizzard blew in and covered her under a foot of black dust. Her lungs filled up and she suffocated. They found her the next day, the same day her family was burying their eldest daughter who'd suffocated a few days prior. I think Kissoon has dinner ready. Nyah, we hope you like shepherd's pie."

Luckily, I did.

Twiggy and I extended our visit with her family until dusk. We ended the evening with the question: Who is Lulu and what does she want?

20
The Masterpiece
Nyah

Without saying a word to each other, Twiggy and I lugged my portfolio into the gallery. Miss Kayte saw us and motioned us to her office. "Hello Twiggy, Nyah," she said, closing the door behind us. "Say, how's your mother, your granny, and my sister?"

"They said they had coffee with you while I was in San Francisco," Twiggy said.

"Yes, we did. We read about the success of your concert, my dear. What a wonderful talent you have."

"Mum said I have talent?"

"Your mum loves you, my dear," Miss Kayte said, deflecting Twiggy's question.

"Do you like my new outfit?" Twiggy looked as if she felt hot anger when Miss Kayte said that her mother loved her. "The Emporium in San Francisco had it in the window, and I couldn't resist. It's the newest 'Frisco fashion."

Miss Kayte kept silent while checking her scheduling calendar.

Twiggy sported a jade green, quarter-length-sleeve blouse with a small white collar close to the neckline and matching white cuffs. Her jacket was hemmed at the hip emphasizing her small waist with three large apricot-colored accent buttons. Her creamy mid-calf capris showed off her calves and ankles. Her earrings were gold loops. And I was wearing new denim jeans from Penney's and a cotton shirt worn open over a white T-shirt and my slip-on loafers with no stockings.

Mister Gilles joined us a moment later, wearing a dark suit with a white shirt, a blue-striped tie, and brown Florsheim shoes. "Hello Nyah, Twiggy. We're excited to see your work," he said, as he carefully laid out my paintings from my portfolio.

"Nyah, I'm speechless," said Miss Kayte, gaping at the array.

"This one here, well, oh my," Gilles exclaimed. "This is, well, a great piece."

"It's a masterpiece, isn't it?" Twiggy asked.

"Let's take a look," Miss Kayte said, smiling.

For what seemed to me to be an hour, Gilles, Miss Kayte, and Twiggy studied each piece of my work without saying one word to each other. At first, I thought they found my work disappointing, and were searching for a kind way to tell me I hadn't fulfilled my promise to them, to produce the work they were asking of me. But as time passed, I realized the opposite must be true.

"Please, excuse us for a few moments," Miss Kayte said, finally. "We'll talk over what we want to do."

Miss Kayte and Gilles stepped out into the hallway and shut the office door behind them. I ran my quivering fingers through my pony's ass haircut. Twiggy held my other hand tightly.

"They like your work, Nyah," Twiggy said. "What's wrong with you? Your hands are clammy. Your forehead's sweating. Haven't you been eating? Sit down."

"I haven't been eating much. Only a sandwich once in a while."

"It's Lulu, isn't it? She's been appearing to you. Nyah, this situation is past being serious. When did you see her? What does she say to you? What is your attraction to this phantom?"

Miss Kayte and Gilles stepped back into the office and shut the door behind them. Gilles was rubbing his thumbs into the palm of his hand. I continued combing my fingers through my hair.

"Nyah," Miss Kayte said, "this indeed is a special moment for us—for you and Twiggy, too."

The idea that my work was good slowly dawned on me for the first time. The relaxed, confident feeling I had while painting each detail of Lulu, the corners of her lips, the sparkle I dotted into her eyes, the easy and smooth strokes of my brushes. My stomach gurgled. Miss Kayte took in a long breath and let it out slowly.

"Nyah, it's a rare occasion, indeed, when Mister Gilles and I agree on anything when it comes to artistic talent—actually, your particular artistic talent. Don't get me wrong, we're dazzled by your work, but Francis is a bit reserved and, you see, a miser of sorts, and I think you know what I mean." Miss Kayte flashed a quick wink toward Twiggy.

Gilles coughed slightly, rubbing his fingers into his white handkerchief and swallowing. "Nyah, you've indeed pleased me. Miss Kayte and I, we're quite excited. Indeed, I could have wept when I first viewed these portraits, all of them. They're all quite different portraits over time of the same subject, well, of Lulu. This portrait here is stunning, simply stunning. You've brought her to life. I feel the mystery peeking around the corners of her eyes. The magical way you enhanced the sparkle in her turquoise eyes make it seem her eyes follow me as I circle her portrait."

"This portrait," Miss Kayte added, gesturing to a painting, "is very different. There's a furrow in her brow, her eyelids are tight, and her jaw appears tense, too, as though she was, well—angry. I like it. I love all of them, each of them shows a different side of her. The exciting color combinations and directional brushstrokes, her luscious strawberry hair and firm mouth, her sweater of many colors, are wonderful.

"And the background feels like an integral part of this piece, it's simply inspired work. Viewing her, I feel joy and sadness at the same time, a tingling runs down my spine. This portrait of Lulu is vibrant, alive, and your choices of color in the various parts of her face, her cheeks, the shadows, and light, they're unique. You used enough subtlety to make her life believable, and yet her face holds the secrets of her soul. Doesn't it, Francis?"

"The difficult techniques you used with your washes, it all blends in so artistically with her clothes and the stunning, varied colors of her locks of her hair," Gilles offered.

"Your washes give the entire portrait a deep and wonderful transparency," Miss Kayte said. "I've not seen such a technique before. It appears as if you added drops of water to her clothing and parts of the background. You've moved the paper at different directional angles to encourage harmony as the water runs and pulls the subject and colors together. This technique brings the entire portrait together in harmony, a loose harmony. How did you give her multicolored sweater so much texture and fluidity?"

"I allowed parts of the portrait, during the first wash and the second wash, to run through the existing wet sections of the wash with no assistance from me. With the pigment broken up by the flow of water, when it dries, these unusual patterns form. Where I would've liked to have more texture, I dropped salt here and there and let it dry and gently brushed the salt away. This section, here on the bottom of her multi-colored sweater, I used crumpled wax paper and smashed it down while the wash was still wet, set a magazine on it, and let it dry. I gently lifted off the dried wax paper."

"She's magically come to life in front of my eyes," Miss Kayte said. "This is the very first time I've felt the passion and the energy of a portrait, and it's the most incredible lifetime experience for me. Thank you, Nyah."

Unable to take all this in, I rambled on, "I used strokes of ultramarine blue, translucent orange for this touch of warmth near the color of her sweater. I dropped here and there turquoise genuine to give the impression of a button on a cardigan."

"This is a new way of watercolor painting," Gilles said. "It's much like impressionism, and yet the image of the girl leaves a question, a wonderment, of who is this lovely girl—woman—almost a spiritual connection, I would say, yes, I would say. We've never received a masterpiece in our gallery before."

Miss Kayte interjected when she saw a tear form in Gilles' eye. "Your work is important. We wouldn't know how much your work is worth, frankly. The point is we're going to arrange for private showing. We've got contacts in all the important museums across the states. We plan to invite the major movers in our art community, including private collectors who will be chomping at the bit to buy your portrait of the girl."

"We'd like to take your paintings on consignment," Gilles said. "Yes, and we are prepared to advance you . . ." He cleared his throat and swallowed. "Advance you, say, fifty dollars."

Quick to respond before I took his offer, Twiggy said, "Private collectors will pay premium price and even battle each other to possess these portraits. You can see this one here," pointing to *With Freckles on Her Cheeks*, "in particular is museum quality, Kayte."

"Always the businesswoman," Miss Kayte replied. "Yes, Twiggy, this portrait is especially worthy. We can advance you say, sixty dollars, Nyah, it's an honest price."

I felt Twiggy looking intently into my eyes. Gilles was rubbing his hands together, and rubbing his thumb into his palm, and his face burned crimson. I kept my direct gaze on Miss Kayte's steady, steel gray eyes. My knees rattled; my heart pounded against my eardrums. I slipped both hands into my pants pockets and secretly pinched myself.

Sixty dollars. I didn't know if Kayte offered me that much money because my work was good or because Twiggy and Kayte were shirt-tail relatives, but Twiggy began packing my paintings, including the main portrait of Lulu, and the other paintings back into the crates. Clearly, Twiggy was intent on saying no to the sixty-dollar advance offer sitting on the table.

"Nyah, we offer you seventy-five dollars," Gilles blurted. "We have to sell at a profit, you know. I suggest you take our offer under serious consideration."

"No matter what you decide," Miss Kayte said, "we'll have your private showing organized before the end of this month. We'll be in contact with you."

With my portfolio under her arm, Twiggy graciously left the office and closed the door behind us.

"Nyah, I promise you the private sector, and more importantly, a museum, will pay more just to have it hung in their establishment. Although Kayte's offer is low for the portrait of Lulu," Twiggy told me, "take Kayte up on arranging for your private showing. You won't be sorry. Trust me on this one, my dear. You appear to not be in the proper state of mind to make this decision alone."

"What are you saying?"

"Let's put the paintings in the car and go back inside and take them up on their offer of arranging a private one-woman showing," Twiggy said. "They'll be delighted, and you'll one day soon be a well-known artist. You're not a starving artist anymore."

21
And the Spider Bit the Fly
Nyah

Returning from the grocery store, I was cranky as hell. I had a burning desire to break every single one of my paintbrushes. As promised, Dave had left me two more space heaters, which took some sting out of cold out of my room. I hung up my coat but kept my thick gray sweater on. I stashed the bottle of Darigold milk in the refrigerator along with a stick of butter, a can of tuna fish, a jar of mayonnaise, a wedge of cheddar cheese, a six pack of Coca-Cola, and I put a package of Oreo cookies in the fridge to keep the mice at bay. I'd found out too late, always too late, that the Delmonico' mice also loved Oreos. I put the teapot on my one burner stove and retrieved my cleanest dirty teacup out of the sink and rinsed it off. I found a teabag in the lunch sack Mary had prepared for me. And, as to not waste food, I ate the rest of the roasted turkey sandwich she'd made for me.

After I ate, my body was too limp to work. My fingers and toes tingled, my breathing labored, and my heart beat faster. Dizzy, I sat in my chair and rested my dogs on the wooden stool next to a space heater. I held my teacup with both hands jittering, just to help steady my grasp, and sipped my hot jasmine tea, spilling some on my lap, but the hot tea didn't burn my leg. The wind was squeaking through one of the cracked windowpanes. Then, I saw in a flash, a movement. I set down my teacup and inched my chair to the window for a closer look.

My roommate, a large, hairy, black and white spider, crawled out from underneath the windowsill. A pair of enormous front-facing black eyes stared at me straight on. When I moved in even closer, it crouched like a cat. The massive front eyes swiveled up and down, side to side, forward and back. It focused its shining dark eyes on me like a pair of binoculars. Having lived at the rooming house for a couple of years, I recognized the spider, an eight-legged Zebra Jumper. I moved my index finger toward the side and the back of the spider. Its smaller fixed eyes detected my movement. It jumped, flipped around, crouched, and stared at my finger. I moved away my finger.

A sudden motion caught its attention. It lost interest in me. The creepy creature fixed its eyes upward. Its mammoth front-facing black eyes swiveled until it located its prey. Once its dinner was in focus, it spun and faced its meal, and hunkered down in full stalk mode. A small insect was snagged in the sticky silk of an abandoned spiderweb.

Quickly, it attached its dragline to the windowsill and jumped seven inches straight upward. It missed its prey and fell downward, landing back on the windowsill. The safety line attached to the Jumper prevented it from falling to the floor. Once again it crouched on the sill, jumped seven inches upward, and this time landed just short of its prey. With its forelegs extended it leaped on the insect. It opened its jaws and deeply bit into its prey. It wrapped it in the sticky silk of the web. Once fully trapped, the Jumper opened its jaw, exposed its fangs, and injected venom into the thorax of its victim, paralyzing the insect.

The spider regurgitated digestive fluid onto the fly which caused its innards to quickly liquefy. The Jumper viciously tore off its head and wrapped it tightly in the silken web. It injected its fangs into the thorax and sucked its liquefied innards into its belly.

My teakettle was whistling. I stumbled over some canvases on my way to it. The chill in my room penetrated my scalp, the roots of my hair were standing on end. My fingers were stiff as I went back to work, and my charcoal pieces and India ink pens dropped to the floor several times. In spite of my foul mood, I was able to draw from memory a few quick sketches of Lulu.

I recalled the curves and lines of Lulu's face as though I'd taken a photograph. I closed my eyes and clearly envisioned her eyes, which I was able to capture with my turquoise genuine watercolor. The way I painted her eyes, with a slight curve in the corner of one eye, it seemed to me I caught a tiny glimpse of her ancient soul. I was able to catch her sadness and her loneliness in the other sketch. I couldn't get the memory of that little girl out of my heart or out of my mind. Nor did I wish my memory of her to diminish. If not for the ragdoll she left behind, I would've seriously questioned my sanity in relation to the evening in the mysterious park setting. I clearly heard the melancholic tune she hummed.

22
Chimacum House, Built 1905
Nyah

On the first day of spring, 1950, the weather was warm and humid, and the sun was shining. Having passed my written and practical driving tests, I pulled up in the driveway at 5530 Hadlock Street with Twiggy sitting in the passenger seat of my Starlight.

Twiggy said, "Did I tell you the surrounding neighborhood has dubbed this house The Haunted House on the Bluff?"

"No, but thanks for the warning."

The boundary of the property was a broken-down stone fence. The steep and winding driveway wrapped tightly around a derelict apple orchard on the east side and ended at the faded dilapidated picket fence. Bleached by decades of summer heat, the fence enclosed the entire structure. The thirteen windows in the round turret reflected the western sky like cut diamonds flickering in the afternoon sun. The chipped clapboards and front door were washed-out green and framed in faded pink. Thick blackberry spines twisted around the railings and slithered upward into the rafters. The ancient house had been broken from exposed torrential gales that sliced through the Strait. Yellow dandelions, overgrown green and purple clover patches, and sprawling perennial crab grass grew to the edge of the escarpment. At the bottom of the hundred-foot drop-off were the jagged boulders of the Strait of Juan de Fuca.

The eyes of the three and a half-story turret peered between the two graceful arching stems of the weeping willow trees as though staring perpetually down into the saw-toothed sea. The unrelenting waves eternally crashed into the solid sharp fractures of the towering stone wall; the blackened, serrated rocks at the bottom of the steep crag never had an opportunity to dry in the sun. The collision of the cloudy green water formed constant opaque salt mounds which clung to the piled-up century-old broken trees left behind by the remnants of the Port Townsend lumber mill. The menace of Thunder Edge heightened the forsaken aspects of the Victorian house. Nailed to the front of the house, on the right-hand side of the front door, was an historic broken-down commemorative plaque with the inscription: *Chimacum House, Built 1905.* In a kid's handwriting, the words "*the haunted*" were written in faded red paint above *Chimacum.*

Oh, God, I thought.

"Oh, look!" Twiggy said. "Look at the two crows in the trees. No, here comes more. I count thirteen. A *murder* of crows."

"Please, Twiggy, I'm creeped out enough."

Oh, *God.* What was I getting myself into? A murder of crows homesteading the trees of my haunted house. *Really?*

"Neighbors used to tell the story about walking past the property and hearing the creaky wooden screen door bang against the frame. And other times, before dusk, the howl of the wind was like the wail of a haunted child."

"God, Twiggy. How do you know those kinds of things?"

"Must be all the brutal murders I've covered since I was a teenager back when I was a cub reporter for Mum. I guess it got under my skin—writing about the violence humans are capable of—the malevolent minds of psychopaths."

After a moment of taking in the disturbing view from the backyard we walked to the deck and clanged the tarnished brass ship bell with the iron rapper. A wide-hipped middle-aged woman opened the gigantic front door and greeted us with a grand smile. She walked with a cane, carrying a packet of papers and an ink pen, which she secured behind her ear.

"Welcome." The woman spoke with a happy lift in her soprano voice. "Hi Twiggy. Your mom says you're doing well. This must be Miss Nyah James, your artist friend. Hi Miss James. My name's Wanda Goss, and I'll be showing you around the estate."

"Call me Nyah."

"Wanda, so how have you been?" Twiggy asked.

"Fine."

"How's the hubby?"

"He's okay. Getting over a cold," Wanda said, as she coughed a couple of times and spit into her hanky. "This is a wonderful house. I think you'll be fascinated. It was built in 1905, you know. The only remnant of the old orphanage is over there by the broken-down fence. See the stones sticking out of the long grass?"

"The stones look like decrepit tombstones," I said.

"Oh, come on, Nyah, stop trying to make the house haunted," Twiggy teased.

"Well, err, um," Wanda stuttered. "Nyah's right on. The stone fence is indeed from remnants of the orphanage's old graveyard."

"What?" Twiggy exclaimed.

"They *are* broken tombstones. Let's go inside, shall we?" Wanda squeaked, quickly shutting out the old graveyard.

Wanda said, "Welcome to what we hope is your new home, Nyah. Let me take your coats."

"Yeah, thanks, Wanda."

She hung the coats in the hallway closet lined with unpainted cedar shiplap. A fire burning in the round-stone fireplace on the north side of the grand room filled the space with the scent of hickory.

"The stones of the fireplace were hauled from the beach at the bottom of the bluff," Wanda said. "Locals call the bluff Thunder Edge. Originally, this house was called Chimacum House."

"Are you sure the stones weren't gathered from the graveyard?" I asked.

"Yes, I'm sure." Wanda answered.

Twiggy poked my ribs.

I noticed a yellow pack of Old Gold cigarettes sticking out of Wanda's purse lying on a windowsill, and a wrinkled Milky Way candy bar wrapper was next to the pink glass ashtray. I counted five cigarette butts, one still burning.

"Wow, this is a mansion, a rickety old mansion, but a mansion for sure." I was astonished by the beauty of the faded fifteen-foot ceilings in the humongous rooms.

"The floors are solid oak planks cut at the Port Ludlow Lumber Mill," Wanda told me. "The doors and floors need a cleaning and waxing, but of course, the house has been empty over forty years. You'll have quite a bit of cleaning and painting to do."

The clatter of our shoes as we inched across the oak floor echoed in the vacant room and the scent of oak lingered from the days of old. The front windows faced west to the sea. The expanse of the raging Strait of Juan de Fuca peeked between two weeping willow trees.

Twiggy took my hand. "This is a beautiful space. The living room is huge. And look, Nyah, look how large the dining room is."

I nodded. I found no words to speak. I was enamored. Spellbound. A welcoming energy, a sea breeze, wrapped around me. A quietness, peacefulness, about the old house. It was quaint with its six-inch-wide windowsills that had enough space on which to set my finished and unfinished watercolor paintings.

Wanda said, "The previous owners left some furniture including this old grandfather's cuckoo clock."

"The sound of cuckoo clocks—*tick tock, tick tock*—always makes me aware of the passing of time," I said. "Grandfather clocks aren't my thing."

Wanda said, "Making us aware of the passing of time is what clocks are for."

She walked to the cuckoo clock and twisted the key, winding the clock. "There you go, Nyah. It's an eight-day clock so you only need to wind it once a week." Ignoring my statement about the clock, she gave the pendulum a little push starting the movement of back and forth, clicking away time. *Tick tock. Tick tock.*

The dining room had the original built-in oak China hutch, a table with ten chairs including captain's chairs, one at both ends, and thirteen large bay windows facing south and west to the sea.

"Did the previous owners leave the table and chairs too?" I asked.

"Yep," Wanda said. "One day the family just raced out the front door and were never heard from again."

"What do you mean?" I asked.

"No one knows why they suddenly packed up and left," Twiggy said. "I remember reporting about it."

The kitchen was colossal, with plenty of counter space for what I imagined: a large spice rack, any number of colorful red and white flour and sugar canisters. And it had a huge walk-in pantry with a door.

"Look, Nyah," Twiggy said, "the pantry door locks from the outside. There's an old skeleton key in the locking mechanism. Kind of creepy."

"What's creepy about it?"

"Mum has a lock on the outside of her pantry door," Twiggy said.

"Why would she have a lock on the outside of the pantry door?"

Twiggy's face paled and her neck was blotchy. She left the question unanswered.

"Look Nyah," Wanda said enthusiastically, "the drainboard has the original cream-colored tiles bordered with turquoise back-splash slate. You'll have a lot of space to be creative with food. The Frigidaire icebox and wood-burning stove come with the place, honey. However, I could have them hauled away."

"I might want to keep the stove, if for no other reason just to keep the kitchen nice and warm in the winter. I've always wanted to bake bread in a wood-burning stove. I can almost smell the yeast."

"Here's a bathroom." Wanda pushed open the door. Under the window was a claw-foot white enamel bathtub, a toilet, and a pedestal enamel sink.

Wanda paraded us around the circle from the kitchen into the living room and the dining room and back into the kitchen.

"You have a large closed-in back porch, as well," she said, starting to pant for breath.

The room looked more like a Halloween horror movie than an old porch. A crusty spider web, stretched and broken by the wind blowing through the cracked window, was weighted with gray dust. In the corner near the back door was a green Maytag hand-cranked wringer washing machine and a rotting ten-foot rope clothesline attached from wall to wall.

"The washer still works," Wanda said. "I'll make arrangements for it to be hauled away unless you want to scrape your clothes with this old washboard and yank your laundry through the rollers."

"Don't think so. Not in this lifetime," I said. "But I do want to keep it."

Twiggy said, "Let's see the upstairs, okay, Wanda? Come on, Nyah, be brave."

Twiggy and I were getting a bit giddy, like two schoolgirls playing in a backyard. We sprinted down the hallway hand in hand. When we reached the second-floor staircase, Twiggy grabbed onto the oak ball on the railing and swung herself around and up the stairs, two stairs at a time with me in tow. Using her cane, Wanda followed us one step at a time while she huffed and puffed.

"Nyah, there're five bedrooms up here," Twiggy said, her voice filled with excitement.

"Yeah, and each has a round-stone fireplace and a bathroom," Wanda added, finally reaching the second floor. "Follow me."

She escorted us into the bedrooms and bathrooms. I could hardly believe each bedroom had a wood-burning fireplace, some facing the sea. The rest had a view of the birch trees and apple orchard.

"This entire floor's a library with built-in bookshelves from the plank floor all the way to the fifteen-foot ceiling. There's lots of books. Come look." Wanda picked up a book. "*Sonnets from The Portuguese*, Elizabeth Barrett Browning, 1850, first edition. *Idylle Saphique*, written by a French woman, Liane de Pougy, in 1901."

"Let me see that book, Wanda," Twiggy said. She took in a deep breath and blew the dust from the top of the pages. Wanda sneezed twice, coughed a few times, and spit into her hanky. "I've heard of this novel," Twiggy said. "This was reprinted sixty-nine times in the first year of publication. It's the first Sapphic novel ever published. But it was never published in English."

"These books belonged to the previous owners," Wanda said. "Local lore has it that the lady of the house wrote a journal while living here."

"Since the family moved suddenly," Twiggy said, "maybe we could find the journal amongst these books." She gently put the book back where she found it. "What's behind this door?"

"It leads to the attic. I doubt if there's anything up there at all. You don't want to go up there."

"Come on!" I said, giggling. I grasped Twiggy's hand and slowly opened the door which squeaked. The stairs were steep and sooty.

"Come on, Wanda," Twiggy said, smiling ear to ear. Wanda followed one step at a time, huffing and puffing.

"The light switch is at the top of the stairs," Wanda called. "Be careful, the stairs may be a hazard."

The unpainted wood stairs creaked with each of our footfalls; there wasn't a handrail to grasp onto. Twiggy was behind me, pushing me forward, giggling. I presumed, by the thick layer of grime on the stairs, that no one had trod those thirteen steps in decades. When I flipped up the light switch one small, grimy, sixty-watt lightbulb dimly lit up in the middle of the attic. The light cast long shadows on several spider webs leading to the rafters. The smell of aging organic material stuck in my nose, the same choking odor found inside an antique furniture store, like the Just as Good as It Used to Be Antique Boutique. I took in a quick breath when a brief wisp of cold air whipped past my face and lifted up the hair on the back of my neck.

"*What was that*?" Twiggy asked, grabbing my arm.

"Don't be trying to make my house haunted, Twiggy. Twiggy, my ears just popped."

"Is it usual for that to happen, Nyah?" Wanda said.

"No, it isn't usual. The first time my ears have ever popped was in the park when the little girl was around."

"Interesting," Twiggy said. "That's the only time? When the little girl appeared to you? Let's take a peek around. Maybe your ears will pop again."

"I'll wait for you two downstairs," Wanda said, wheezing as she turned away.

"Okay," Twiggy said. "We'll be down soon."

The attic was surrounded by six gable-shaped coves, and the window panes were covered with dirt and grime blocking out daylight. The walls were layered with flaking wallpaper of red roses surrounded by baby's breath with honeybees flitting.

"Here's another door," Twiggy said.

The heavy door was on the west-facing cove. I opened it and saw a large bathroom with wallpaper matching the room's wallpaper. An enamel claw-foot tub, a toilet, and a white pedestal sink with a chip near the drain had a black spot the size of a tarnished silver dollar. In front of the west window was a two-foot-long copper captain's telescope facing the sea. A feeling in the room, a timelessness, like a *déjà vu* moment, waved over me. I pressed the hairs down on the back of my neck. Twiggy took my hand and guided me to the window facing the lake and the sea beyond.

"I need a deep breath of the salt of the sea," Twiggy said, unlocking the swing-in double windows and pulling them open. "The front yard ends at the bluff with a drop-off of over a hundred feet. Legend has it, during a rare winter thunder-snowstorm, two tiny sisters who lived in the orphanage toddled between the weeping willows, stopped at the edge. Hand in hand, they leaned forward, and because of the wind, they fell to their glory. Legend has it that when they leaped to their deaths, the sound barrier cracked and shook the ground."

"There you go again with your stories of legends and folklore."

A rush of cold wind blew back our hair; the skin on my arms goose-pimpled, and the sea smelled of pungent kelp. We breathed in deeply, bursting our lungs with the strong breath of the sea. Twiggy put her arm around my waist and kissed me softly and deeply while she stroked my cheek with the tips of her fingers. Her warm tongue mingled with mine, and my passion spread to my thighs. Her mouth was soft and gentle. She kissed both of my eyes while she pressed me against the wall. I had an odd sensation—like fear—but I wasn't afraid. I was falling in love.

Twiggy whispered, "I can't keep my hands off you, your silky skin, and your soft wavy hair."

I felt my cheeks warm. Twiggy and I lovingly necked and pecked each other, pressed into each other. She spread my legs with her knee, unbuttoned my jeans, and slipped her warm hand between my jeans and skin, my wet, waiting, private area. As I was about to orgasm the double windows slammed shut.

"How weird. Let's go downstairs, and now," Twiggy whispered, removing her hand gently from my pants.

We quickly left the room and barreled down the stairs to the first floor. Wanda was sitting on the front room window seat crushing her Old Gold cigarette into the ashtray.

"Where do I sign?" I asked.

"I think you'll be startled to know the price of this great house. Twiggy, Junior, suggested I sell this house to you for a very low price. A steal. I could offer you a six-month tryout. Let's talk about signing papers in six months."

"Thanks. How soon can I move in?"

"Any time, my dear, and it's I who should thank you. I had the power turned on for this showing, so you'll need to put the electricity bills in your name. You'll need firewood delivered and a telephone."

The cuckoo clock sounded: *cuckoo, cuckoo, cuckoo.*

23
Not A Friend in The World
Nyah

The lunch crowd was at half capacity when I arrived at the Sequim Bay Restaurant, making it easier to decide where on the mural I'd resume my work. Suzie, the darling she was, kept me supplied with hot orange blossom tea and fresh lavender honey.

"What's wrong with her?" Suzie asked, pointing at the red-headed girl I'd drawn nursing a full glass of Coca-Cola at the counter. Her elbows were draped on the counter with her jaw resting on her palms. Her pale face was partly facing away, eyes staring out the window past the snowfall toward the bay.

"What do you mean?"

"She seems she hasn't a friend in the world. And she looks sick."

I saw what Suzie meant. Something about the way I'd painted her eyelids, half closed like she was losing the strength to keep them open. Her shoulders rounded forward, her back was curved. I felt an indescribable grief looking at her. I'd painted a truth about her, about Lulu and about the half-hidden mystery I felt deep down in my soul to be Lulu as she would someday be.

Roger edged up behind Suzie and commented, "Yeah, I like her. Throughout the years many a lost soul has come into this establishment from the cold to get warm. This one appears like she's peeking into her future and her prospects seem to be as bleak as her past."

"If you two don't mind," I said, "I don't feel well. I'm heading back to the Delmonico and see if I can get some rest."

24
My Name is Lulu, Plain Lulu
Nyah

At the Delmonico bar, I brushed away the raindrops from the shoulders of my coat and sat on a stool, two down from Mary.

"Dave, will you make me a hot Grand Marnier, please?" I asked. "I still have money."

"Coming right up, Nyah," Dave said. "You look tired."

"When I walked by yer room I heard a woman's voice behind the door," Mary said. "Sounded like she was talkin' ta someone. Or talkin' ta herself. I'm not sure."

I shook my head. "I don't have friends."

Mary crossed her arms virtuously. "I told ya I heard a woman's voice." She spat her chew inside an empty Folgers' can. "She must a let herself in." Mary chewed Skoal when she was off work and chewed Adam's clove gum working the café.

"Okay, thanks." I wondered if Mary often stopped at my studio and pressed her ear against my door.

"Here," Dave said, "take your drink upstairs."

Intrepidly, I trudged up the flight of stairs. I had no friends, other than Twiggy. And Twiggy was at the *Gazette*. Having a woman in my room waiting for my arrival was unheard of.

I pushed the door open. My ears popped. Something was wrong, something was out of place. I felt the energy. I knew without a doubt that Lulu was in my room because my ears would pop when Lulu was nearby. But Mary said a *woman* was in my room, and Lulu was nine years old the last time I saw her. My heart pounded. My knees rattled.

I flipped up the light switch. And there she was. Lulu sitting on my hard-cushioned armchair with her long curly strawberry hair draped down the back of the chair. She sat primly in front of one of my easels with a half-finished painting set on it. Her shoulders were back, her hands crossed in her lap, and, surprisingly, her feet touched the floor. I stood there for a moment looking at her. My stomach churned butterflies; my knees spun into rubber.

"This painting of me needs more work, don't you think? Nyah, how do you paint my features so well without me sitting for you? Don't you want me to sit for you, Nyah?"

Lulu called me Nyah, not Miss James. She hadn't called me by my first name before. I meandered over to the window and faced the woman in the chair. She wore a tanned leather jacket, unzipped, showing a tie-dyed T-shirt with a tan-colored vest. The jacket had leather fringes at the breast, sleeves and the hem, and her black leather boots reached her knees. On her neck she wore multicolored beads and around her head was a colorful band. What an odd outfit, I thought.

"Lulu, where'd you find those unusual clothes?"

"Mostly at secondhand stores. We all wear them. Do you like my bell bottom pants? We're the hippie generation. Do you like my outfit, Nyah?"

"How'd you find me?" I asked, ignoring her question. Frankly, I wasn't interested in her peculiar clothing fashion, nor the definition of a hippy generation. The dim light highlighted creases at the edge of Lulu's turquoise eyes and two frown lines on her brow. The edges of her mouth sagged slightly, the way a thirty-year-old woman's mouth droops due to gravity drag, starting with a mere hairline wrinkle on each end of her lips.

"Oh, Nyah, you're unhappy to see me," she said, all the while considering my room. My face burned. My living space was untidy and in shambles. Not knowing what to do, I pushed my sable brushes to a corner of the table and picked up some of my dirty dishes and stashed them in the sink. The sink's white enamel was stained with different colors of paint left behind from rinsing my brushes.

"Would you like some tea?" I asked. "I have some orange blossom tea here somewhere."

But she was more interested in scrutinizing my apartment, glancing quickly at the scruffy furniture, the dusty windowsills and floor and all my canvases scattered throughout the room. She took a long look at my unkempt bed which consisted of two crumpled yellow-white sheets and my Indian blanket slung halfway onto the floor. One of my grungy slippers was half under my bed, the other not visible. Lulu's eyes widened, clearly startled by my messy room. I was mortified.

"Your room's nice," she lied. "Orange blossom tea with lots of fresh honey sounds fine."

I rinsed out my teakettle, dent facing the wall, filled it with water and set it on my hotplate.

"This room's awful, Lulu, and dirty, too. I really haven't paid attention to anything in here except my paints, ink and canvases," I said as the back of my neck prickled.

Lulu stood, took off her brown leather gloves one finger at a time, removed her jacket and laid it over a chair. "Where's your dust rag? I don't know where to begin."

"Lulu, under no circumstance are you going to clean this room."

But she wouldn't take no for an answer. All I could find was one of my old painting smocks with every color in the rainbow permanently stained into the cloth. She pinched the smock by the shoulders and shook it three times. So much dust was released that she coughed a couple of times. She flitted about the room wiping away dust and picking up random debris and heaped the mess into a pile near the end of my bed. The teakettle whistled and spat. I poured the hot water into our cups and dropped a couple of orange blossom buds in each and with one of my two teaspoons I dripped golden honey into each cup.

"Lulu, our tea's ready. Please, stop cleaning."

Instead of sitting at my cluttered table, she took the teacup and sat on the floor in a lotus position facing the lineup of my landscape paintings.

"Come sit with me," she said, turning to me. She had dirt on her face from rubbing her chin. "Where'd you paint these? They're lovely. You're a good artist, you have talent. Not everyone who paints has talent, you know? I don't think I've ever visited these places."

"They're views I remember of a childhood up on a hill in the woods." I sat on the floor next to her, holding my knees close to my chest.

"You know, it's interesting how sometimes I look at paintings or drawings and even though I know I've never been to those places, my soul twinges and my heart yearns, and soon my travels take me right to those places I never knew."

The heavy gray sky sparked and rumbled and proceeded to dump buckets of cool spring rain. A light breeze blew onto the windowpane. Coming in from the sea, a riverboat softly sounded its lonesome toot.

Lulu set her teacup on the floor between us, rose and picked up a drawing and walked to the window. She was in a dreamy state. Then she came back to me and clasped my hand. The warmth of her touch caused my hand to jerk away from her. I leaped to my feet. I noticed how stained and faded the four walls were, how dark were the spider webs clinging to the four corners of the room. Lulu noticed, too.

"Where's your broom?" she asked, setting the painting on the floor. "Or should I ask, do you have a broom?"

"No, I don't have a broom. Let's have another cup of tea."

She sat down at the table. "Yes, I'd like another cup of tea. Thank you. How's your mural coming along at the restaurant?"

"I finished it yesterday. It's a really good painting, if I do say so myself."

"Has the art gallery bought any more of your paintings of me?" she asked. "Would you like me to pose for you?"

My heart jumped at the chance. My work on her portraits would be finished more quickly having her present and sitting quietly. I also hoped she would drift into another reverie while I studied her, surveyed her hands, her lips, her turquoise eyes, anticipating the discovery of her enigmatic soul.

"Yes, I'd love that."

"May I come to see you when the sun rises?" Lulu asked. "Or I'll sit for you as soon as I can."

"Sure, whenever you can."

"Will you be happy when you get rich? You'll be rich, I'm sure. Perhaps we'll meet again when you're rich and famous."

"I just want to paint."

"I think you'll be quite content to paint freely without the strain and fear of not having a morsel of food on your table. You were in fear when I first met you. Nyah, do you ever wonder about the mystery of a world which learns too late, always too late? And why life blooms, then rots?"

I watched her face. Her eyes watered. I held out my hand. My heart felt squeezed. "Take my hand and you won't feel so sad."

"You're not sad anymore, Nyah?"

"No. When we first met, I was cold, afraid I was going to die in the storm. I was lost."

"We're never lost, Nyah. Although we can lose our direction. I've learned I feel lost when I'm most lonesome. Have you felt the same?"

I was nervous and edgy. The room seemed different than it had an hour prior, like something was going to suddenly change. The rain was still plinking on the windowpane. My room was dim and lifeless, but something was changing. My ears were ringing and making a popping sound.

Lulu handed me her empty teacup and the teapot. "Here you go. We're finished with our tea. Wash the dishes before you forget. I'll wait for you."

"Oh, by the way, what's your last name?"

"My name is Lulu, plain Lulu."

I washed the dishes and set them on the drainboard on top of my flour sack rag. I dried my hands with the edge of the rag. My ears popped.

"Lulu?"

But Lulu had vanished. Her brown leather gloves were gone, too. The more surprise visits I'd had, the less my mind tried to make sense of the phenomenon named Lulu. My mind now completely accepted the presence of Lulu, the illusionist.

25
English Leather and Flipping Pancakes
Nyah

A few days after I signed the legal papers giving me ownership of my haunted mansion, I realized I was putting off packing my easels, paintbrushes, and India ink bottles even though the weather had warmed, making a nice day for moving. But for some reason I was reluctant to leave, to move out of the creaking chilled room that had been my shelter for over two years.

A knock on my door startled me. I had already paid Mary my past due rent and Twiggy was working at the *Gazette*. I had no idea who'd be wanting to talk to me. I opened the door a crack and there stood Dave.

"Dave, hi. Wow, come to see me off?"

"To wish you happiness in your new house and to give you a few empty Olympia beer cases to put your things in," he said. "I thought the boxes would make it easier for you to pack."

"Yeah, I guess they would. I was just going to grab stuff and toss everything in the backseat of my coupe."

"No, you weren't," he chortled as he stacked several empty Olympia beer boxes in the middle of my room.

"Yes, I was."

"Well, today you'll be packing in style. When you're all done let me know, and I'll help you carry the boxes down to your car."

"Thanks, Dave. Give me an hour or so."

"Okay, I'll be waiting."

After I filled the beer cartons with my meager belongings I sat on the rickety bed for a moment and said my so-longs to the rundown room. Now the room didn't look so ratty to me. Likely because my possessions were crammed inside ten cardboard boxes, and my paintings and new canvases, wrapped in newspaper, leaned against the wall.

The spider web was still attached to the one and only sixty-watt lightbulb which continued to swing back and forth in concert with all the air leaking through the window. The broken-down Frigidaire clanged, and the steam heaters clinked. The hairy black and white Zebra Jumper crawled out from beneath the windowsill, its massive black eyes swiveling up and down, side to side, forward and backward. Focusing on me like a pair of binoculars, it hunkered down in full stalk mode.

"Shit, I am so out of here." My words echoed against the walls of the empty room.

After sliding the boxes down the flight of stairs and stacking them in my Starlight, I approached the One-Eyed Dog to say goodbye to Dave and Mary, but stopped at the bay window and peeked in.

Seven red-faced, bearded Irishmen were at the bar, some sitting on stools, others standing, resting one foot on the brass footing, all with a hand on a glass of foamy, cold Olympia beer steins, and oh, yes, the one-eyed Irish setter they called Blinky lay on the plank floor next to the brass spittoon.

Mary stood at her blackened cast-iron gas grill, its yellow flames flickering. Her white bib apron was wrapped twice around her skinny waist and tied in front in a bow as she fried bacon and scrambled eggs. A spatula in one hand, flipping pancakes, her other hand scratching her left breast, she all the while mindlessly chewed clove gum. Her chestnut hair was combed back into a soft bun around which she had tied a blue-ribbon.

Dave strolled across the room, heading to the walk-in cooler, his blue plaid Pendleton shirt tucked into his faded blue jeans, his sleeves rolled up to his elbows. His hips moved like a cowboy's gait as if he were approaching his favorite horse, steady and self-assured. His white hanky hung out of his back pocket, moving freely back and forth in step with his stride.

Some things never change.

26
The Pussy Catkins Are in Bloom Again
Nyah

I drove my Starlight up the driveway to Chimacum House and stopped in front of the garage. A hot sensation blazed and surged, as if the soul of the house, a ghost of the creepy rundown graveyard, reached out and grabbed me. The field of bramble and thorns acted as a fear-provoking barrier telling me *No Trespassing!*

The weather was changing, and the atmosphere was warmer. Much to my surprise, someone, likely Wanda, had hired a man to clear the cracked concrete path from the driveway to the front door, making it less treacherous.

Outside the yard, in the overgrown kid graveyard, sparse woods of deciduous white birch trees stood forty feet high. The unique, thick, and deeply ridged white bark of the trees was peeling off in long strips, as nature intended, and the enchanted branches were beginning the annual spring sprouting.

Carrying a carton of Olympia boxes, I walked thirteen strides from my coupe to the back door porch only to find the door locked. I left the box on the porch and ventured my way around to the front of the house to view the thunderous sea. Blasts of cold wind lifted my hair off my prickly neck. The eyes of the three-and-a-half-story turret peered between the two weeping willow trees, and the long pussy catkins were in bloom again. Heebie-jeebies crawled across my shoulder blades. When I neared the edge of the cliff, a long fat charcoal gray garter snake slithered in front of me and quickly disappeared under the blackberry thorns.

I screamed!

The two black crows I'd named Mable and Parker perched on a branch of a weeping willow and cawed and made clicking sounds over and over. I thought I heard one of the crows speak: "Run! Run!" I jumped and fell on my back. Got up and ran as fast as I could and leaped three stairs onto the broken front porch. The hairs on both of my arms stood up under my sweatshirt.

Thankfully, Wanda remembered to leave two house keys and a key for the garage under the new flowerpot next to the front door. The card hanging from the pot was from Wanda congratulating me for having agreed to take on the dubious haunted house, for someone finally taking the house off her plate.

I turned the key, heard the latch click, and took in a deep breath. I pushed open the door with the hairs on my arms still bristling, and then I exhaled, hoping to relieve some anxiety. The atmosphere in the room was no longer stale; it had magically turned into the scent of a lavender garden.

In the living room, the stone fireplace was snapping and crackling, scattering hot cinders into the metal safety screen. The scent of dried hickory permeated the room and took me back in time, back to the neighborhood park where I first met Lulu and her red-headed ragdoll.

Warming myself in front of the fireplace, I glanced around the large empty room. Twiggy thought she'd talked me into hiring a man to paint the inside of my house, but I liked the ancient gray and faded lavender colors on the walls and ceilings. At once, I decided to keep the house as she'd been for over forty years. I let out a couple of hoots into the cavernous room. I wanted to hear the echo of my voice bouncing off the walls and high ceilings. A tingling sensation warmed my belly. I was falling in love with my house, haunted as she was.

Footfalls on the front deck sent a panicked lightning bolt up my spine. I watched the glass knob slowly twist. The door creaked open.

"Hi darling," Twiggy said, floating into the house like Lana Turner, chic, mysterious. "Here, help me. Take this lunch basket. I thought you'd be hungry after painting the living room, but I see you haven't bought paint yet. Ah, you're not going to paint, are you?"

Twiggy already knew me pretty well. She glided toward me. Her raw sienna-colored cotton duster blew softly behind her, exposing the front of her light rose-colored cashmere sweater. She took off her gloves and, holding my cheeks, kissed me gently. Hand in hand we sat in the window seat. She wore blue jeans cuffed above the ankle, black and white saddle shoes, and blue bobby socks.

"Nice. You brought lunch, in a picnic basket no less. I love you."

"Let's bring your worldly belongings inside before we eat. I love you."

After we lugged the remaining Olympia boxes inside, we sat in front of the fireplace on two of the chairs left behind by the previous owners.

"Granny's a great cook. She's famous for her fish and chips," Twiggy said. "Let's go shopping tomorrow for some furniture, especially for your bedroom."

"Yeah, especially for my bedroom," I said, smiling. I kissed her neck and her lips.

On the window seat, Twiggy somehow moved into a yoga lotus position with her knees crossed and her ankles neatly secured at the crux of her thighs. I sat next to her with my feet dangling.

"She makes the sexiest tartar sauce," Twiggy said. "She uses fresh dill and chopped baby dill pickles."

Twiggy dipped a piece of halibut in the thick pickled tartar sauce and took a large crunchy bite, closing her eyes, clearly enjoying the taste of the halibut and Granny's tartar sauce. She gently dabbed her wide mouth with the linen napkin Granny had provided.

"Open wide." She offered me a bite of her fish. "Wider."

I parted my lips, preparing for her offering. I closed my eyes. When I felt her fingers on my lips and the fish on my tongue, I pressed my lips on her fingers, pulled away and chomped a large bite of the beer-battered fish. After I swallowed, I felt her lips on mine. Our lips parted.

"Yum. Granny does make sexy tartar sauce."

She gently dabbed my lips with the linen napkin and kissed me again. I pulled back.

She asked abruptly, "You don't like it when someone pays a lot of attention to you, do you?"

"For me it's a thin line between having enough attention and having too much attention," I confessed. "Feeling responsible for someone's trusting love in me—well, it makes me nervous. I'm afraid my lack of, well, lack in a lot of areas in my life, I'm afraid you'll tire of me and lose interest."

"I'm falling in love with you, Nyah. I'm serious. I want to know all there is to know about you, what you believe in, people you admire, places you've been, and places where you'd like to visit. I'm not going anywhere, Nyah. I'm in us for the long run. Are you okay? You're distracted."

"Twiggy, no one has ever wanted me. Nobody *sees* me. Nobody would walk across the road to say hello. I'm a ghost. I know better than anyone that I have no value. I'm invisible."

"Nyah, don't say those things about yourself. It's not true. You're so beautiful I can hardly stay in my body when I'm with you. And you're a gifted artist. You're very special to me. You're my inspiration. And the world is about to see you for who you are. Help me help you to believe in yourself. I believe in you, Nyah."

"The world will see my art. There's nothing special about me."

"Nyah, you have the gift, a special gift."

"I close my eyelids when people pass by, because I don't want anyone looking into my eyes and seeing the nothing. There was one time, years ago, when I looked into a mirror, I looked into my eyes. I saw the nothing and it scared me. Fact is, you already know all I am."

"Nyah, when I was a senior in high school, I had a crush on the homecoming queen. I was always hanging around her. I even wrote a note to her."

"What'd you say in the note?" I asked, taking a small bite of fish and tartar.

"I don't remember. I probably told her she was pretty or something similar." Twiggy dabbed tartar sauce off the corners of my mouth. "Mrs. Abernathy, the girl's counselor, called me into her office. She'd called Mum and told her about my unnatural behavior toward Miss Prissy and asked her to come to school for a meeting."

"Miss Prissy?"

"Her name was Priscilla; her friends called her Prissy."

"What happened? Did they suspend you?"

"The counselor told Mum I'd written a love note on the wall of a bathroom stall, which was a lie. My face burned. My hands were shaking. She told Mum that Prissy felt uncomfortable being in classes with me. I couldn't breathe. I thought I was having a heart attack. I ran out of the office and kept running. I arrived home and ran into my bedroom. Granny followed me and shut the door behind her. She rocked me in her arms."

"Did Granny say anything to you?"

"I have no idea. I blacked out. I drifted far away to parts of the universe unknown to me."

"What do you mean—you blacked out?"

"All I remember is at some point after the meeting with Mrs. Abernathy, Mum put me in counseling with a psychiatrist in Port Angeles, far enough from Port Townsend as to not hear rumors about her daughter being a homosexual deviant, as she put it."

"Oh, my God."

"The psychiatrist told Mum that sexual feeling between two women was abnormal and immoral. His diagnosis was I was suffering from neurosis, and my inclination toward females would lead to loneliness and isolation. Ironically, it did.

"He also said homosexual tendencies would lead me to seducing innocent girls into my lifestyle of deviancy. He strongly encouraged my parents to get me involved with a church and have me baptized in the Holy Spirit. He said the Holy Spirit would cleanse my soul and forgive my sin. The Holy Spirit would magically cure my illness and convert me to heterosexuality, which would, he said, make me a happy, well-adjusted heterosexual. Granny wants to know if you're happy living in this house."

"You went from a shrink diagnosing you as an immoral, sexual deviant to Granny wanting to know if I'm happy living in a haunted house." I chomped down on another bite of fish. "Tell her I need more time to get used to living in a haunted house."

"The past is not a subject I think much about."

Twiggy pushed the fish around in the tartar sauce. "But my relationship with Mum changed after the meeting with the counselor at school. She was embarrassed. I'd shamed her. I've never been able to please her. She and I rarely spoke. I always felt I wasn't good enough for her. Even when I came home with A's . . . 'Where's the A plus?' she'd ask. I don't remember one relaxed moment in her company. I don't remember her ever telling me she loved me. I tried to show her I loved her when I was a child. I'd kiss her goodnight before I walked upstairs to go to bed. When I was six years old, I stopped kissing her goodnight. You see, she never kissed me back.

"I started sneaking up the stairs without kissing her. Midway up the stairs, I'd stop and wait for her to ask me, 'Hey, where's my kiss?' But she never did. Because she never knew I'd stopped kissing her goodnight. I never told Mum I loved her. I thought she'd reject me. So, I rejected her first."

"Speaking of the house," I said, hoping to ease Twiggy's upset, "this morning I rambled around the yard to think about the haunted history of this property. The wind was blowing through the willows. There in the trees was the murder of crows. And the same yellow-eyed owl was on the corner porch railing. It sat there watching me without blinking. Oh, and a fat slimy snake almost knocked me off the bluff."

"Jesus, Nyah, are you serious?"

"Yeah. I don't know how I was able to stay standing, actually. I felt as though someone or something grabbed my coat and dragged me backward. Shit, I sound as crazy as a loon."

"It sounds like the reputation of this place is getting to you, like you hope it is haunted so you can move back into the one-room boarding house and feel safe."

"What are you implying?"

"We bought kitchen supplies, silverware, knives, dinner plates, bowls, and frying pans so you would cook yourself food and eat on nice plates. Have you lined the cupboards and drawers? Do you have your silverware, and dinner plates put away? I'm saying you may be stuck thinking and feeling like you're still deprived. You're not a starving artist anymore."

"When I stepped over the threshold, the house was warm and I felt somehow, well . . ."

"Somehow what?"

"Somehow, the house itself welcomed me. I wasn't afraid, once I got inside and stood in front of the fireplace. Weird huh? This is the best fish and chips I ever had," I remarked, changing the subject away from the house.

"You don't talk about family."

I felt Twiggy challenging me, trying to get to know me faster than I was comfortable telling.

"Like I shared with you before, I don't have family. I was kind of, well, left on the doorstep of a church, I guess."

She stared at me. "Nyah, not really?"

"Really, I guess. Somehow, I was found wandering in the woods. Someone brought me to this town. My past is pretty much blacked out. At some point I made friends with the two elder Irish ladies who own the antique store down on Water Street. I have orange blossom tea and honey with them about once a month. They give me pads of watercolor paper, and other art supplies."

"Yes, our family knows them well, the McGowen sisters. They're former Catholic nuns."

"After the three of us got to know each other, they told me the story about how a pastor found me sitting on the steps of his church wrapped in a turquoise Indian blanket. They said I was about five or six years old."

"Hmm, the closest church is in Chimacum, a few miles out of town, and churches around here aren't known for taking in orphans."

The cuckoo clock clicked—*tick tock, tick tock*—the rhythm of the pendulum back and forth, back and forth. The grandfather clock struck twice, *clang, clang*. The little bird popped out the little yellow door. *Cuckoo. Cuckoo.*

"Yikes, I'd better get back to work," Twiggy said, leaping up. "I have a story to finish, and as I said, Mum runs a tight ship at the paper. I want to know more about you being left on a doorstep of a church."

"And I want to know more about you and your mother, your relationship. When I bring up the subject, you either go silent, change the subject, have an anxiety attack, or leave."

We kissed and hugged each other tightly. As she flew out the front door, she said, "I love you."

A moment later she opened the front door and leaned in. "Oh, I'm leaving tomorrow for a few days. I'm doing the Great American Music Hall in San Francisco. I'll see you first thing when I get back home. I love you! You're my beautiful lady."

I said, "Twiggy, right after the snake slithered into the bramble bushes, one of the crows in the willow tree told me to run . . ."

But Twiggy had already shut the door.

27
Lulu The Feather
Nyah

The following morning, I woke up in my warm and cozy attic studio. After rubbing my eyes awake, I stumbled over and stood in front of the window. Even with the windows closed I heard waves breaking against the jagged boulders before they crashed the shoreline. I tranced out staring at Tibbals Lake. A lifetime seemed to have passed since I'd skated with Lulu.

I pulled open my window. The first of the seasonal robins were pacing the lawn, listening, and pecking for worms. The clusters of catkins were drooping from the white birch branches. The buds were getting longer and the leaves green, red, and yellow. The murder of crows was roosting on a wide area of the branches. My lavender bushes were about a foot high with buds starting to open, and the first bees of the season flitted from one lavender bud to the next. I shivered and shut the window.

My ears popped.

The echo of the sea was no longer audible.

The shadow of Lulu filled the doorway. Her skin was washed out and pale. My face flushed. I gazed unseeingly to the sea and azure sky.

"Are you ready to pose for me today?" I asked, pretending not to care.

Lulu sniffled. "Yes, of course. I thought you'd be happy to see me, Nyah. Are you happy to see me?"

"Yes, naturally I'm happy you're here. How'd you know where to find me?"

"I wanted to see you, to be with you," she said, ignoring my question. "I might as well pose for you. Would you like me to stay? I'm not very pretty today."

I faced her. "I think you look beautiful, Lulu. You seem a bit sad. Are you feeling okay?"

She wept. "Are you in love with your new friend?"

"What? Who do you mean?" I was totally flabbergasted by her question about Twiggy! She actually sounded jealous.

"You know who I mean, Nyah."

Her turquoise eyes were dark and her soul distant, as though she had withdrawn from the room. I feared her emotional absence would harm her portrait.

"How shall I sit for you?" she said, sniffling. "Do you have a tissue?"

I brought her my Kleenex box from the studio bathroom.

She blew her nose. "Thank you, Nyah."

I showed her how I wanted her to sit. I thought the light pink wallpaper with tiny red roses was right for a portrait of Lulu. Seeing the freckles on her cheeks up against the roses warmed my heart. It took me a while to get the light to fall right to enhance her freckles, and all the while she sat there without saying a word, glancing at her alabaster hands neatly folded in her lap. When I was satisfied the light was right, I set my canvas on the easel and sketched the lines of her chin, neck, eyes, and mouth.

I enjoyed the task of mixing pigments: alizarin crimson, cobalt blue, cadmium scarlet, and raw sienna. I loved the scent of raw sienna, like moist dirt. Lulu's face was changing dramatically with each portrait I painted of her. There were moments when I was sure her turquoise eyes changed to green and back from one stroke of my brush to the next.

For some reason, the difference in her eyes worked in my favor. I sensed I was peeking into another cubbyhole of her soul she'd kept hidden. I was filled with a strange exhilaration. My stomach tingled, my heart drummed faster, and my knees felt like rubber bands. My creativity streamed through my brushes faster than I knew was possible. So frantically was I painting, I'd failed to notice the dusk. Without warning, Lulu drooped forward, like a ragdoll. I pounced to her side before she slipped off the stool. But when I lifted her in my arms, she opened her eyes and smiled.

"I'm tired, Nyah."

She was a feather. I helped her lie down on the twin bed and slid my lumpy pillow under her head.

"Take a bit of a nap. I'll get you some water and make orange blossom tea." I tucked my Indian blanket around her.

Lulu lay sleeping when I returned.

"Lulu, I'm setting a cup of hot tea on the stand next to bed," I offered. "I insist you drink it."

She awakened, propped herself on one arm, flipped her long red hair over her shoulder and sipped slowly until she emptied her teacup.

"I feel much better now," she said. "I feel a little warmer. I can pose for you again, if you want me to."

I admit I wanted her to feel better quickly so she could continue her pose. My brush was on fire, and it made me a bit apprehensive to think I might never have such powerful, dynamic inspiration back again—to feel it as strongly as I felt it that day.

"No, no, you need your rest. We have lots of time. Rest a while."

She sighed softly and sniffled again. "May I have another tissue please?"

As I handed her the Kleenex box she said, "No, Nyah, there's not a lot of time, but I'll do as you ask. I'll rest."

Shivering, she lay back and closed her eyes. I tucked her hands under my Indian blanket and snuggled the fringe under her chin. Her hair spread out on my pillow, the saturated colors of scarlet apples, saffron orange, peaches and apricots, and her pinkish raspberry freckles dotting her cheeks. My heart squeezed and released, which felt like fear. Who are you? I thought. What or who has brought you here to me? Are you a lost child or a lost stranger passing through my life? Are you from some story in my past? Those questions ran through my mind as I quickly sketched her face posing in slumber.

I was startled when she opened her eyes and looked solemnly up at me. "You're all I have, Nyah."

She sat up and huddled under my blanket with her slender arms wrapped around her shinbones and her chin on her knees.

"Do you want me to pose for you? You wouldn't be happy if I would never come again?" she asked, uncertainly. "You do wish for me to come back, yes?"

I didn't know how to respond. I needed to paint her because I was getting paid a good amount of money from the gallery for her portraits. I needed her to come back to me again. She must have seen in my face the answer to her doubts, for she smiled and brushed the hair back from her face and lifted her hair off her neck.

"I'll come again as soon as I can."

"Lulu," I choked out.

"Yes, Nyah?"

I edged over to the window overlooking the Strait. With my back to her I asked, "Do you have family? Where do your family members live?"

I thought if she didn't show up in a reasonable amount of passing time at least I'd know where to start my search for her, if I needed her to finish posing for me. The gallery wouldn't wait forever. I turned and faced her.

Lulu shook her head. "What does it matter if I have family or where I live? You can't come to me. Only I can come to you."

She spoke softly and with gentility, but her voice had a tone of finality. For a moment we looked at each other across an abyss of more than the space of my studio. She reached out to me in a vulnerable gesture and let her hand fall to her side. The moment was gone. My intimate stranger, dreaming of I knew not what.

A moment later she slipped off the bed, folded my Indian blanket, placed it at the end of the bed and put on her coat and hat. "Goodbye, Nyah. I'll come back as soon as I can." She looked up at me with tear-filled eyes.

With her hand on the doorknob, she faced me and whispered, "Please wait for me." Her ghostly figure retreated out the door. I felt she could have left the room without opening the door, so ethereal were her movements.

"Lulu, wait," I shouted. I ran to the door, opened it.

Lulu had vanished.

My ears popped.

28
The Man On The Moon
Nyah

During the last days of spring, weariness overtook me. Twiggy was on her way home from San Francisco, via our town airport. In my attic, I sat in front of the fireplace and rested my feet on my ottoman. I lay back on a pillow with my eyes closed. The embers cast a flickering light in the early evening darkness giving the attic an unnatural, eerie atmosphere. My nerves were on the edge of rupture.

Something, perhaps the wind or the bang of a downstairs shutter, roused me from sleep. I rose quickly. Disoriented, I lost my balance. I didn't know where I was at first. I recognized my paintings scattered on the floor and the red-haired ragdoll slumped on the windowsill. Fragments from a dream made my head ache. I recalled an old man hurting me. I looked around my bedroom almost hoping I'd find someone nearby watching me. Bits and pieces of the dream were vague images only, and as much as I tried, I wouldn't allow my awake mind to correlate them. The breeze rattled the attic windows and the sound of white birch branches scratching at my clapboards—it all creeped me out.

In the dance of the flickering light and shadows, I walked to my window and pulled it wide open. The wind quickly dried my cheeks. My anxiety had grown more intense as each day passed living alone in Chimacum House. The sea was towing my soul into itself, out to the end of the horizon. The whitecaps, even on such a dark and windy evening, could not be blackened. From high above Thunder Edge, I heard waves crash and break against the razor-sharp rocks. A heavy spring fog rolled in from the Strait onto shore and crept up the slope of my yard. Goosebumps rippled up my arms and down my legs. I was hiccupping. I saw a movement. Someone wearing a long dark coat and a hat with a wide brim was standing between my weeping willow trees, looking up at me. I strained to get a better look. I rubbed my eyes and squinted to see through the slowly drifting fog. I blinked. The figure was gone. Vanished as though it had never existed. I was drifting into madness.

I was tired. I was frightened. I needed the warm light of spring to wrap her rays around me, a rainbow washing over my insanity. The vague spell of my dream was overtaking me. I stood in front of my mirror. A nebulous sensation was taking form, something not quite remembered, like my dream, as if I were waiting for someone. I was about to move away from the mirror when my red-rimmed eyes caught movement in the reflection. Something—someone—ran past my bathroom door in the dark. The presence of another person creeping around sent me into full-blown panic.

The scent of lavender wafted past me. I pressed down the small hairs standing at my hairline. Danger and fear sank deeply into my chest and ran up my spine. My heart pounded the sides of my neck. The presence was real. Someone was watching me, waiting for me, skulking from the shadows. I crawled to my armchair and dreamed.

The woman in my dream touched me. Her fingers were ice, my face burned. The woman leaned over my face and kissed me. The face was Lulu's, Lulu was the shadow under the tree. I let her kiss me again and we soared over the Strait of Juan de Fuca hand in hand with a soft breeze blowing back our curly red hair.

Although I fought the urge to stir, I couldn't stop myself from awakening. I was in a daze. I felt the weight of my Indian blanket. I moved closer and held Lulu in my arms. I felt her body warmth next to mine. I realized I was holding my pillow against my heart. My pajamas weighed heavy on my body and were soaked from perspiration. I was suspended between two worlds, the unreal world of burning desire and the world of edgy reality. I opened and rubbed my eyes.

My ears popped.

"Nyah, wake up, sleepyhead," Lulu said from the other stuffed armchair near the window. She was wearing a V-neck pullover tunic top with gold, red, black, pink, and beet red colors splashed together with a matching belt, and white, flare-legged pants. Her pointed shoes looked like they were half shoes and half boots. They were made of pieces of blocked leather. The vamp was bright cadmium red, the heel raw sienna, and the sides up the toe were the color of hooker's green. Her shoes had a low heel and came up to the top of the ankles.

"Lulu, when—how—I mean *why* are you here? Or are you in my dream? I had a dream about you."

"What you had was a dream with me, not about me."

"What do you mean?"

"I mean what you think was a dream wasn't a dream at all. You were in a state between dream and reality—the bridge of trance—but, of course, they're the same thing, dream and reality. We're actually engaging with each other, and now you're awakened sufficiently to relate with me on your level of consciousness. How do you feel at this moment?"

"Bewildered. Tangled."

"Never is our world—our worlds—what they seem to be. The fact is, dreams are another word to describe another reality."

"You talk in riddles. I don't understand you. Who are you? Why do you pay me so much attention and take up so much space in my thoughts? You can't possibly be real. You're an enigma from another world."

"Nyah, speaking of another world, I've witnessed a miracle. Americans have planted an American flag in the gray, powdery surface of the moon! When the astronaut, his name is Neil Armstrong, first set foot on the moon, he said, 'That's one small step for man, one giant leap for mankind.' Do you know the moon is 240,000 miles from Earth?"

"Lulu, again you don't make any sense. It's impossible to fly to the moon."

"It's not impossible. Before the astronauts prepared to return to earth, they wrote on a plaque, '*Here men from the planet Earth first set foot on the moon—July 1969 A.D. We came in peace for all mankind.*' I love you, Nyah."

"Jesus, Lulu. I love Twiggy. Stop saying you love me! Please stop!"

"Twiggy! *She* doesn't love you. She loves herself. She has nothing to offer you. I can offer you whatever you wish for. I can keep you safe. I can take you places where you've never been. I can give you the power to do anything you wish, to go anywhere you desire in a blink of your eye. I'm offering you riches beyond what you can imagine. I'll make you famous. I offer you my love, forever love.

"Has it ever occurred to you to ask yourself why you think the sun rises each morning to a new day, instead of rising upon the old day all over again? Have you ever wondered how much of what you do or think or believe are your own thoughts? Or is it possible your thoughts and beliefs are part of how your brain was wired in the womb of your mother?"

"I don't know what you're trying to say to me." I sat down on the end of my bed to get a better view of Lulu in my armchair. I wrapped myself tightly in my Indian blanket. "You're confusing me."

"You think there's only one road, one direction, the direction you have been told since birth. And your mind accepts what you were brought up to believe. You think God is a mystery, you think the universe is a mystery. I suggest that you don't think about the mysteries of existence very much. You plug along like a work mule. You don't really believe God and the universe are mysteries at all. You're afraid of everything."

"I want to be right where I am. I'm happy with who I am," I said decisively, "and I love Twiggy and Twiggy loves me."

I blinked. Lulu vanished.

Vanished!

My ears popped.

To be honest, I admit I am fearful of everything. My fears, on the other hand, were formless, making me feel afraid of what I didn't under-stand. I was afraid to fall asleep, and once asleep I was afraid to wake up. I was trying to decide which was harder to bear, my feelings of fear or my sense of desolation. Emptiness swallowed me.

My world was a silent, empty place, like an abandoned piano pushed into a corner of an attic, an instrument with spider webs intertwined between the hammers and the wires, the piano itself waiting for someone to find her and once again touch her keys with passion, play the harmony between her notes, the empty space between the striking of one key and another key making harmony resonate in the human soul. I was sucked up in my own helplessness—my self-pity—and at the same time, I heard my voice screaming as if through a tiny hole on the top of my skull.

In every room in my haunted house, I heard a distinct echo bouncing off the walls—the sound of time passing, *tick tock, tick tock*. The grandfather clock ticked away time.

29
Clitorotica
Nyah

On a spring evening, Twiggy and I lounged in the living room, snuggled together on her soft white couch under a pink flannel. Twiggy clasped my hand in hers. "Nyah, let's go upstairs."

I held her warm hand and together we danced up the winding staircase. I was filled with anticipation, my imagination taking hold of my body and my soul, shivers up my thighs and down my arms to my fingertips. Her bedroom was white and pink silk everything, the wallpaper, rugs, sheets, and pillowcases. The upholstery on her bedroom furniture was overstuffed cloudlike silk.

Her bedroom suite faced Discovery Bay and an epic, hazy view of the snow-white Olympic Mountains. The queen-size bed was neatly laid out for us. Twiggy pulled open her double pane windows. A spring storm flashed lightning over Discovery Bay. The chill filled the room instantly, the cold seared my cheeks, my lips were on fire, and my thighs sizzled all the way up inside my inner minora labium to my clitoris. Not only was I starving for deep intimacy, the tenderness and affection of mutual love, my soul was being born again.

With no hesitation, Twiggy leaned down and gently nipped my lips with her teeth. "I can't wait."

We kissed each other. Together we gasped. I wrapped one of my legs around her waist and moved my tongue deep inside her mouth. Warm wisps of sensation shot to my core. Twiggy, with no hesitation, slipped my sweater over my head and let it fall to the floor.

My nipples stood erect, pressing into my camisole. She lifted my camisole over my head, and she gently filled her mouth with one of my breasts.

I groaned. The fluttering sensations shimmered in my belly. I slipped off her camisole. Her breasts were beautiful, full, and they welcomed my eager mouth. I suckled one of her nipples while caressing the other with my hand. She pressed her bosom gently into mine and moaned in my ear.

"I want you, Twiggy."

I started to unzip my slacks, but she said, "Let me, darling."

She let them fall to my ankles. She gently moved me onto the silk sheets and lay on top of me, all the while opening my lips with her own, kissing me deeply. She kissed the sides of my throat while she caressed my breasts. I was intoxicated by her touch, her warm breath on my skin. Another burst of lightning flashed overhead, then a crash of thunder rumbled across the dark waters of Discovery Bay. She ran her hands over the curves of my hips and feathered her fingers down my spine. I gasped and shivered. I moaned as she circled her tongue around my nipples.

"I love your warm tongue touching me, Nyah," she whispered, in my ear.

She straddled me and placed her knees on either side of my hips, leaned down, and kissed me, a moist kiss, devouring my mouth for several minutes. She entwined her fingers inside my own and put my hands above my head, which left me willingly vulnerable to whatever she had in mind. She suckled each of my nipples, gently, then a bit more aggressively. I felt her wetness, her womanhood, on my thigh. I was breathing heavily. My heart was beating inside my ears.

She let go of my hands and kneaded my breasts, very much like kneading bread, very gentle, and kissed and suckled my nipples until my ecstasy was so great, I started crying. I grabbed tufts of her hair and bit my lip as the sensations of her touch flooded my vagina. Her hair smelled like rosebuds. I rolled her over onto her back, ran my tongue across her stomach, and continued with my wet tongue to her inner thigh. I put my head between her legs and caressed inside her private, sensitive area with kisses. She lifted her hips in motion with my tongue. My legs quivered.

My breath was quickening.

"I love you, Nyah. I have dreamed about this moment since I first met you."

Twiggy put both her hands on each side of my cheeks and lifted my face close to hers.

"Straddle my head, Nyah. I want to lick your wetness, hurry. I need to taste you now. Move closer, rest your knees around my ears."

I leaned forward and steadied myself against the headboard. My private area vibrated like a high E minor chord as she licked and kissed me. I felt my own wetness. I rolled on top of her and positioned under over my mouth. She watched me as I moved my head up and down with my tongue deep inside her. Together we shuddered as the tension grew stronger and stronger.

"Nyah, faster. I need you now."

I slipped her soft body gently down until her lips were licking and kissing the inside of my thighs, and with her wet, hungry tongue inside me, almost instantly we orgasmed at the same time. I had no idea such sounds of pleasure could escape from my innermost soul.

Twiggy whispered, "Are you okay?"

I crawled on top of her and kissed her and tasted my own sugar on her lips. I slid my tongue down her belly and inside her most sensitive area between her legs. I and gave a light tug on her clitoris with my teeth and gently licked deep into her vagina.

"Oh, Nyah!" Twiggy moaned and lifted my head up to hers. There we lay in each other's arms.

The curtains snapped from a gust of wind.

30
The Summer of 1938
Twiggy

One chilly night in November of 1937, I, Twiggy Carpenter, met a lovely woman named Jennifer at the La Paloma nightclub in Miami, and we fell in love. During the summer of 1938, the La Paloma was stormed by nearly two hundred women and men garbed in hooded Ku Klux Klan robes. They assaulted the entertainers and customers, ransacked the establishment, and robbed the cash register. And they burned a fiery twenty-foot cross on public property. Customers were arrested and shoved into paddy wagons and taken to county jail and booked on charges of indecency and immoral behavior.

My time in county jail was the most humiliating and terrifying event of my life. The cops dragged me out of the paddy wagon in handcuffs and shoved me into a small room where I was ordered to undress and put on a striped black-and-white jumpsuit and jailhouse slippers. The cop, who was male, stood in front of the stripping room and watched while all of us disrobed. My jewelry was taken from me, along with the contents of my purse, including cash. I was given my one telephone call. I called Mum.

After I told her where I was and that I needed bail, she said, "Shit, Twiggy!" before slamming down the receiver.

Still with hands cuffed in front of me, I was pushed into a communal shower. I looked for Jennifer, to no avail. The water was cold and dribbled out of the showerhead. The matron cop directed us to wash our entire bodies with a bar of Ivory soap which included scrubbing our hair and our *twat*, as the matron grossly put it. I was humiliated. I covered my pubic area with one hand. The matron cop yelled at me to use both hands. The red face of shame engulfed me.

I felt a bout of diarrhea burning in my bowels, an urge I couldn't contain. The contents shot out of my hind end like a water hose spraying the white tiled floor and walls. I nearly fainted from shame. A frantic ruckus broke out. The matron cop shouted for help. Three guards arrived and escorted the other inmates out of the shower room. I was ordered to clean myself. After I rinsed off, I was ushered into the dressing room and ordered to dry my hair and put on black and white coveralls. I ran the towel through my hair. It snarled and stuck out on all sides of my head.

They handed me a cardboard box containing a roll of toilet paper, one washrag, a bar of Ivory soap, one small tube of Ipana toothpaste, a makeshift toothbrush which was a simple plastic stick with a small sponge glued to one end of it, and a blanket looking much like a horde of moths had eaten away at it. The female side of the jail was noisy—women crying, screaming at the jailers and calling them cunts and bitches. Women whistled and made smacking sounds with their lips as I passed by the rows of cages on the way to my cell.

As iron bars slammed shut one by one, I burst into tears. When the last cell door closed with a crash, I was stunned to see one toilet, one sink, dirt, litter, and five women. With my back to the bars, I froze.

31
Northern Ireland to Ellis Island
Twiggy

After I'd returned home from my concert at the Great American Music Hall, in San Francisco, Nyah and I dined again at the Sequim Bay Restaurant. Susie and Roger told us their mural was becoming a popular attraction for diners as far away as Port Angeles. After partaking of the delicious meatloaf special, we drove to the drive-in movie, located in a cow pasture just south of town. The movie playing was *All About Eve* starring Bette Davis. After the movie we drove to my beach house for a nightcap. I slung our coats on the bench inside the front porch and we kicked off our boots.

"How about a glass of chardonnay, or would you prefer a merlot tonight?" I asked.

"Chardonnay, naturally," Nyah answered. "Do you mind if I wait for you in your piano room?"

She was sitting on the piano bench when I arrived with our wine. "Can you play?" I asked, realizing it hadn't occurred to me that she might know how to play the piano.

Nyah said, "Hmm, I've never even sat down at a piano before now. My childhood is a mystery to me. Alvena and Roseyl told me I was an orphan a long time ago."

"An orphan? That's mysterious. How would they know that, I wonder?"

"It turns out they knew my mother. They said she was a rosy-cheeked seventeen-year-old when she sailed alone from Northern Ireland to Ellis Island."

"I'm curious as to how Alvena and Roseyl would know a single thing about your bio-mother, let alone that she was rosy-cheeked seventeen-year-old."

"Apparently, in the 1920s, the Ku Klux Klan re-emerged in Washington state after the war. They said my mother rode a bus, along with other Irish Catholic immigrants, heading for Seattle with a late-night stopover in Spokane, in eastern Washington. The Klan stormed the bus with police batons. When the station opened the next morning, they found a barefooted Irishman hanging by the neck on a low tree branch. He'd been shot and hanged. There was a sign attached to his jacket with some sort of an Irish slur painted on it."

"Holy shit. What happened to your mother?"

"Alvena told me that during the raid, she was raped and left for dead, but she didn't die after all. Sister Roseyl said she was taken to a Catholic nunnery in Seattle. During her stay, a doctor examined her and determined she was pregnant. After she gave birth to me, she disappeared somewhere in Seattle and was never heard from again. The sisters at the nunnery took care of me until I was six years old, then they sent me to live with a family in Port Hadlock, but the family had wanted a baby, not a six-year-old. So, they dropped me off inside a Catholic church in Cape Flattery. I ended up running away, which left me destitute, living in attics of deserted houses at night, and begging for dimes and nickels on the streets during daylight."

I said, "Granny and Claudia are close friends of the McGowen sisters. It's odd they've never mentioned them having taken care of an orphan. Although, they were involved with the orphanage before it burned down."

"Interesting." Nyah looked into the fireplace flames. "When we were telling your family about my finding little Lulu in the park, Claudia and your granny were looking at each other as though they knew a secret no one else knew."

"I noticed their glances, too. But we'd been talking about that little girl, not about you being an orphan."

"But the little girl, Lulu, told me she was an orphan," Nyah said, reminding me.

"This Lulu mystery is getting deeper and more frightening the more information we get," I said, the hairs on my arms prickling.

32
My Corvid Family
Nyah

The attic door leading to my studio creaked when I pushed it open. I plugged in the space heater, and it plinked while it heated. The air was stale from all the years of being unoccupied, I guessed. I pulled open the window facing the Strait of Juan de Fuca. A cold breeze blew across my face whipping my hair back behind my ears. The silver-topped waves crashed on the craggy rocks. A group of screeching gray and white seagulls dove in and out of the sea. One gull with an oyster in its beak flew into the sky and hovered over a large rock before letting the oyster go. A direct hit cracked the mollusk wide open. A few dozen squawking seagulls flew overhead hoping to reap the spoils.

I liked the original faded walls in my attic, the peeling wallpaper with tiny faded red roses surrounded in baby's breath and honeybees flitting. And I loved the long ceiling windows beaming bright light into my studio. I emptied the cases of my painting supplies onto the floor. Then I noticed the red-headed ragdoll sprawled over a pile of rags. I picked it up and set it on the windowsill. I heard a noise on the other side of the room.

I quickly spun to see the studio door closing in slow motion; it slammed shut with a bang, vibrating the room. With caution, I opened the door. No one was on the stairwell to the second floor, and I heard no one downstairs. I closed the door and leaned against it, one hand over my heart.

A breeze from an open window must have slammed the door shut, I told myself. But I was left with an uneasy suspicion that the breeze had nothing to do with it. My chest muscles tightened, and my breathing was labored.

"Get out of the house and take a hike on the beach," I said out loud. I put on my coat and headed out the front door facing Thunder Edge.

The homesteading owl was perched on the rail at the end of the porch. I followed the side path to the isolated seashore. I slid sideways on my butt at least halfway down to the beach. The shore of Thunder Edge was laden with razor sharp-edged boulders ranging in size from six to fifteen feet high and as wide. I glanced behind me from time to time to see my deep footfalls in the wet sand. Dark green-gray kelp heads floated onto the shoreline, old campfire ashes blended with the ash gray sand, gulls shrieked overhead against the gray sky, the strong, yet sweet smell of seaweed made me sneeze.

I picked up a few sand dollars and put them in my pocket. A menacing fog from the horizon blew over the beach. I noticed cracks and large holes in the melting ice which had formed in the shaded puddles behind some of the boulders, a sure sign of spring, but there was still a chill in the air. I pulled my wool cap around my ears and tightened my scarf around my neck.

My logical mind struggled with the fact Lulu had aged exponentially in a few weeks. She appeared to be about my age at her last visit. The mystery surrounding her made me question my sanity and at the same time, I'd hoped to see her again. Part of me was attracted to the phantom that called herself Lulu. It seemed enough for me to believe that wherever in this wide world Lulu belonged or longed to be, she would soon come back to me. To be in her company again was clearly not in my control. Nothing was in my control.

I pondered the three little words Twiggy said to me as she flew out my front door: *I love you.* Her expression of love pressed on the back of my mind. A panic rolled around my stomach and up into my heart like the waves crashing onto shore. Her words freaked me out. Part of me thought she was flirting, but flirting wouldn't have set me into a panic. Flirting seemed safe to me. Something in the way she said *I love you* . . . It told me she meant exactly what she'd said.

Twiggy Carpenter in love with me? She could have any one she wanted; I had nothing to my name except paint brushes, watercolor paper, lots of paint tubes, India ink and pens, some cold hard cash, and a very hot Studebaker coupe. Oh, and lest I forget, a haunted house. I hadn't bought a lick of furniture, having decided I wouldn't need, nor did I want, more furniture. A twin bed in my attic studio, a davenport, and a stuffed chair were all I was used to having.

The afternoon mist drifted to shoreline moistening my skin, and the ancient sea crashed and splashed, drenching me. The din of gulls squawking, bald eagles screeching, the acrid sniff of kelp and the thunder of the surf all acted in concert with my spirit, letting me know all was normal. I felt content to do nothing except wander the beach, to weave in and out of the sharp boulders, to let my mind mingle with the fog.

I was shivering from the cold wind while I trekked back up the slippery path. A few spots of snow remained on the side of the path which was less slippery than the mud path. I took hold of bush branches next to the path that enabled me to continue up the slick path without falling. I reached my two weeping willows on solid ground.

The sound of a creak in a loose board on my porch gave me the creeps. Mable and Parker perched on the corner rail. Mable was standing on one foot and cocking its head toward me. Again, I thought I'd heard one of the crows speak. "Run! Run!"

Suddenly, I saw it: a dead black snake with a thin white stripe. slung over the porch railing—an offering from my corvid family. A spring cloud passed over the lake. In its light I saw, on a branch in the middle of one of the birch trees, the bold yellow eyes of the Pacific Northwest Great Horned owl.

33
Lulu Lives Here?
Nyah

In an altered mental state, I walked from my attic studio down to the library on the second floor. I'd remembered the diary Miss Roseyl gave me to read, left behind by the woman who'd once lived in my house. I found it lying on the bookshelf.

"Good morning, my love," Twiggy said, as she entered the library.

"Hi, honey."

"I'm making coffee and will be right back. Sound good?"

"Yes."

A few minutes later the nutty scent of Hills Bros. coffee drifted up the stairs into the library with Twiggy ahead of it.

"Thanks, Twiggy. I could use some hot coffee this morning. How'd you sleep?"

"I didn't get much sleep, if any at all. Yesterday was a rough day. You didn't sleep either, did you?"

"No. I'm going through a lot, but I'll be okay. Let's sit on the old davenport. Are you ready to read the diary with me?"

We sat and stared down at the pages for a few moments. I read out loud where they had fallen open. Twiggy cuddled up with me under a blanket.

> *My husband and I have determined this house to be haunted. We hear someone pacing the floor in the attic at all hours of the night. From the driveway, sometimes we see several of the windows in the turret are open and on other days we find them closed and locked.*
>
> *What I am about to write will sound like I'm a lunatic. Be that as it may, the two black crows that perch on our rail speak*

a few English words. I personally have heard one of them say "hello" and "goodbye." Then one day my husband heard a crow say, "Get out, get out."

There is a spirit living in this house. Sometimes I feel an icy breeze when I pass by the door leading to the attic, a breeze that blows my hair upward. The hackles on my dog's neck rise all the way down her backbone to the end of her tail and she stands at the attic door and barks wildly.

Sometimes when I am outside working in the gardens, I see a small girl with red hair standing in the open window. She wears a smock of some kind covered with paint smears. I blink and the girl disappears.

My husband and I have decided to pack our belongings and leave. We will drive as far away from this house and this town as is possible. Woe to the person who buys this house.

"It seems you're not the only person to have Lulu sightings," Twiggy said. "Now we know why this house has been empty for over forty years."

"Lulu lives here."

"What do you mean—Lulu lives here?"

"It's what I think." I felt the pressure of being grilled. Deflecting her question, I said, "Twiggy, I'm so lonesome I can barely get up in the mornings."

'Nyah, I too am lonely. It's getting harder for me to be away from you." Tears formed in her eyes. "I've been wanting to ask you to move into my beach house with me."

"Are you saying you're thinking of retiring from your career?" I asked, not quite believing I'd heard Twiggy ask me to live with her.

"Yes. I'm tired of the lifestyle, being on the road, living in hotels; it's dangerous to be a lesbian out in the world. I just can't believe all the violence against us, just because we love women."

"Twiggy, let's go to bed and snuggle."

34
We Must Believe in The Absurd
Nyah

As I sat at my picnic bench on the balcony, cuddled in my Indian blanket facing the sea, the North Star was in clear view; the infinite blinking points of light filled the sea of black effervescence. Remnants of flying stardust exploded the heavens. One thought in particular held me hostage: we as humans must sometimes believe the undeniably unbelievable. We're faced with an infinite, endless universe which we accept, because our imaginations are incapable of visualizing this unfathomable truth: there's no image in the furthermost limits of our imaginations of *infinity*. We must believe in the absurd.

My ears popped.

A voice from behind cracked me out of my trance. "Are you enjoying your new home?"

I stopped breathing. From the darkness of the doorway, Lulu stepped forth. She was dressed in a red, orange, and green ankle-length tie-dyed dress, a style I hadn't seen before, and a soft pink cashmere sweater buttoned at the top. A multi-colored headband circled her forehead and was tied in back. Her brown leather-strapped sandals were the same type Jesus was depicted as wearing in old paintings.

"Lulu!" I shouted "You've got to stop sneaking up on me like this. A sudden voice coming from behind me in a dark room, well, who knows what might happen?"

"Nyah, I've missed you. Why do you talk so harshly to me? I might think you're not happy to see me."

Not only were Lulu's clothes different, but little about her did I recognize. The look in her eyes was changed from a week earlier. Her countenance was so different that my first thought was how I must paint her before she changed expressions again.

"Lulu, you're different from when we last met. You seem more mature, and I've never seen clothes like what you're wearing. What's hanging on your necklace?" The icon looked like a two-pronged pitchfork set in a silver circle.

She glanced down at her dress and sandals and smiled. "I love this dress. These clothes are very much the fashion nowadays." She touched the symbol on her necklace. "This is what we call a peace sign."

The look in her eyes changed. "Of course," she said sadly, "you don't know of the events I've seen as of late. Our world is in chaos. We're in another war. Our president's been assassinated, President John F. Kennedy."

Lulu covered her face with elegant hands. Her breathing labored. I held her in my arms. Her shoulders heaved.

"What do you mean?" I asked, holding her at arm's length. "We're not at war, and President Truman hasn't been assassinated. Who's John Kennedy?" Her shoulders were rounded in toward her chest. She sniffed several times. "Please don't cry. You're mistaken about a war and our president."

She pushed away from my hug. "These are things you're not as yet aware of. Have you not guessed I'm a traveler through time? A seeker of knowledge? I move through atmosphere and upon the earth. I see that which you have yet to see."

"I suppose I've had thoughts about who you are. But I don't know what you need from me. A time traveler? What's a time traveler?"

"I thought you surely must know what I want from you after all we talk about. I'll sit for my portrait."

"No, frankly, I have no idea what you want from me. I don't even know if you're real." I examined her more closely, and I jumped at the chance to paint her. "Do you mind if I take off your headband? It's making your hair flat."

I noticed she had a look of pouting around her eyes. "Lulu, are you okay? Are you upset? Would you like some tea? The kettle's on the stove."

"I thought you'd be happy to see me. Are you glad to see me? Yes, I'd like some tea, Nyah, dear."

I didn't have the heart to ask if we could continue with her portrait. Blood drained from her cheeks, she frowned and was twisting a strand of her red hair between her thumb and index finger.

"I tell my new girlfriends about you. I tell them you're beautiful, and you're painting me and you're a great artist. When I say you were almost starved to death when I met you, they laugh. One girl thought my story was romantic because I told her how you met me."

"Romantic?" I asked, handing her the teacup and saucer.

"They think I'm in love with you. They're correct, you know. I am in love with you, Nyah. Since the first time we met, I've been in love with you." Her voice faltered and the freckles on her cheeks paled.

"Lulu, I'm not in my right mind when you're around me. I feel the warmth of your hand, I see your vivid turquoise eyes, and I can smell the yellow roses in your hair. But, when you utterly disappear from my presence, I question my sanity. Sometimes I wonder if Twiggy doubts my stability."

"Are you angry with me?" Lulu asked, expressing hurt in her furrowed brow. "I don't think you like my clothes or the way I wear my hair."

How she cast down her eyes and stared out the window was attractive and mysterious and added to her appeal. Her expression was the look I wanted, her mouth pouted, the corners of her lips twitched.

"No, I'm not angry with you, Lulu. Actually, I'm flattered. But would you mind sitting for me for a while?"

"No, I don't mind." She sat down, her chin nearly resting on her chest, clearly dejected.

"Nyah, would you be angry if you find out you love me, too?"

I was holding one brush in my teeth while I painted with the other. "Will you please look into the light?"

"Why haven't you ever asked me why I have creases on my brow, crinkles you didn't see the last time I came to visit you? I look different to you, and you look the same to me."

"Lulu, you're in a strange mood today." I swished my brush into my light burnt sienna wash. "You've been hinting, telling me there are things to come I'm not aware of. You see future events. Frankly, I have mixed feelings about you. When I'm painting you, I feel affection, and when you vanish, I feel fearful."

"Oh, Nyah, are you saying you love me?" she asked, with a meaningful inflection.

"I have to concentrate on what I'm doing. You want me to be able to sell my work, don't you?"

I was losing my focus. Her questions were unsettling and taking up most of the space in my head. I was jittery and on edge.

After several minutes of silence, she said, "I feel sad about things sometimes, the things I see, the cruelty in this world."

"We all feel sad about the cruelty of the world sometimes. Mostly we call it anxiety or worry."

"I'll sit still for you. I'll be quiet."

As she promised, she sat silent, unsmiling, absent. She withdrew back inside of herself; I knew I'd hurt her feelings. But her hurt feelings helped me to capture another secret pearl of her soul. But Lulu was in a fidgety mood which made it difficult to concentrate on the important details of my work. She got up and strolled around the studio and glanced out the window to the sea.

"My friends and I march in the streets all over the globe. We carry signs saying we want peace and love. A few signs read, *Make Love Not War* and *Free Love*. And we smoke marijuana and hash and drop LSD. Sometimes I like being a part of a community, being around people my age who have the same values. But sometimes being a part of a community of like-minded people, well, it's frightening. Do you know what I mean?"

"No, not really," I answered. I was barely listening to her because I was focused on my painting, especially the areas around and behind her eyes. I'd hoped I could find the window into Lulu's soul—to catch a quick peek into what was unknown to me.

"There's a place in New York called Greenwich Village. A place where like-minded people gather in bars, places called gay bars. Police are raiding these bars and violence has erupted. My friends have been beaten and arrested. One of my friends was killed by a policeman when he beat her with a billy club."

For some reason watching Lulu change from a mere freckle-cheeked child to a middle-aged woman in six months didn't send me into a panic. Perhaps because I'd not yet allowed into my psyche the possibility of my being a stark-raving wacko.

"I want to make you something to eat," Lulu said. "Do you have any luncheon foods in your refrigerator? How about a bologna and Swiss cheese sandwich? I'll butter both slices of bread and cook it under the broiler. It will help the cheese melt."

"I'm not sure if there's much in the fridge. I've lived here for two days and haven't bought much food. There may be milk and bread."

"I'll be right back. I'll run downstairs to the kitchen and make you lunch. Would you like a glass of milk?"

"I'm pretty sure I have a can of tuna in the pantry," I said weakly after the door had shut behind her.

About a half hour later Lulu stepped into my studio looking paler than I'd seen her. Her posture was slumped, and her tie-dyed dress dragged on the floor in front of her.

"I found some mayonnaise, so I made you a tuna sandwich. I want to cook for you, you know?" She set the lunch tray on my desk and sat on the davenport. "Stonewall Inn."

"What do you mean? Stonewall Inn?" I'd been so involved with painting around her eyes, I hadn't been listening to her stories.

"The gay bar where the riots were, where we were being beaten and arrested. It's not safe to be different from normal people, Nyah.

Garbage cans, garbage, bottles, rocks and bricks, broken windows, more blood running down the broken street."

Lulu shifted her stance and looked out the window toward the Strait of Juan de Fuca. She was half asleep.

"Lulu, I'm getting tired. I'm going to wash my hands. Please sit on the davenport and wait."

I had to take a moment or two to think about the stories she was telling me. Her tall tales about the future unnerved me. I shut the bathroom door.

I splashed water on my face and brushed my teeth. I was about to spit the toothpaste into the rainbow-colored porcelain sink when I saw one furry black leg, and another furry black leg stick out of the drain. Those two hairy legs gave one short lunge and up came a huge black spider. I took aim and spit out the toothpaste, but my aim was off. I twisted on the hot water as high as it would go. The black spider curled up in a ball and rolled down the drain.

Back in my studio, Lula was gone.

A note was taped on my easel.

I ebb and flow,
I go and go.
I'll follow you,
Wait for me when I do.
My years are long,
You are where I belong.

35
With Freckles on Her Cheeks
Nyah

It was the Fourth of July, the first day of the New Moon cycle, when I saw Lulu again. At the very least, I was sure I saw her in a moment of time. Miss Kayte and Mister Gilles had scheduled my *Miss Lulu* private showing for the holiday, and my exhibit would be open to the public for the following five days. Included in my showing were forty-eight watercolor and India ink sketches, and four full-scale portraits of Lulu in various moods.

I'd been able to paint her when she felt joyful, happy with the way she was living her magical life, during those times when she appeared, seemingly out of nowhere, with her heart full of wonderment and love and a soft twinkle in her eyes.

Then without warning, her personality would dramatically transform into a dark and wounded soul, the vulnerable orphan who struggled to be sovereign but was forced to go it alone in this ever-altering, complicated world. In the other full-scale portrait of Lulu, I was able to capture her damsel personality—Cinderella during the ball—and transformation—embers to ashes. The star of the show was my larger-than-life portrait of the magical Miss Lulu that I called *With Freckles on Her Skin*.

Surprising to me, the gallery was crowded. There were collectors from around the country. I admit during my show I was getting increasingly tired and confused—feeling lightheaded, distracted, and more than a tiny bit crazy. I was on edge, mostly because I never knew when or if or where Lulu would appear to me. Her unannounced sightings left me frazzled. Therefore, what follows I cannot swear to.

The art gallery was so dimly lit, save for the spotlights on my work, that I was unable to trust the information my eyes were receiving. I was walking around the gallery trying to avoid talking to potential buyers when I saw a movement across the room—a shadow. I blinked a few times, then through the crowd, I saw a splash of strawberry hair in front of *With Freckles on Her Skin.*

My ears popped—a sure sign Lulu was about to bring me into her world.

I squinted, hoping for a better view, but the buyers and other folks were effectively blocking my line of sight. I stopped breathing. The shadows and the lights were acting in concert. Manic energy ran up my spine. The crowd shifted enough to enable me to see the shadow magically change into Lulu, the woman. She had her hands to her face, appearing to be crying. I rushed toward her.

"Lulu?" I whispered.

"Hello, Nyah," she said, without diverting her eyes. "You've captured secrets of my heart, my pain. I see these feelings in the way you painted my eyes."

Lulu spun around and held my cheeks in her warm hands and quickly kissed me. Her lips on mine felt unnatural—not of this world. I pulled away and held her at arm's length.

"Don't do that."

"Don't do what?" Lulu asked, pouting.

She was older than when I'd last seen her. She wore a pretty knee-length pink dress with white gloves, and her strawberry hair had grown long past her shoulders. She had parted it in the middle with no bangs.

"Don't kiss me," I said.

"I've missed you. Where's Twiggy?" she asked, ignoring my scolding.

"She'll be here in a few minutes."

"I knew you'd be rich one day. You'll be famous because you painted me. I'd like for you to paint me again as I go through time. Will you?"

"I'm not sure. I need time to think."

"Who knows why two lovers come together?"

"We're not lovers, Lulu."

"I don't have much time with you. I have to travel to another time and another place. I don't know when I'll see you again. Kiss me."

"No, I won't kiss you."

Lulu vanished.

My ears popped.

When I turned, I saw Miss Kayte nod at someone.

"Nyah, we're quite pleased with this showing," she said, with a smile. "Your collection of Lulu drawings and paintings are the rave." She looked at me in alarm. "What's wrong? Are you okay? Where's Twiggy?"

"I'm fine. Twiggy will be here soon."

Gilles joined us. "Art lovers are here from Seattle, Wenatchee, Whitefish, Denver, New York City, San Francisco, and Tucson," he said, with an awed inflection in his voice.

"I admit I'm excited to have my first big show." I glanced around the gallery searching for Lulu.

"Nyah, we're doing very well this weekend," Miss Kayte said. "I have some good news for you, too."

"Did you pass a redheaded woman in the hallway just now?" I asked, completely distracted.

"What? No. Why do you ask? Nyah, you're out of breath. What's wrong with you? Come sit down," she ordered.

I slipped past Miss Kayte and Gilles without speaking, and finally made it to the back door, hoping to see Lulu. But I was too late. Miss Kayte tapped me on the shoulder, startling the tarnation out of me.

"As I was saying, we have the best kind of news for you, Nyah. A representative from the Seattle Art Museum was in the house today. She said your work has depth. She thought it an act of genius the way you gave the impression of Lulu's eyes following her around the room."

"You did what you set out to do, Nyah," Gilles said. "You captured the girl's innocence as well as her depth of mystery, the enigma of her soul."

"Really?" I gasped.

"I told you the girl would make you rich and famous, didn't I?" Miss Kayte said, with a wide smile and a twinkle in her eye. "Here's your payment."

My arms trembled when I reached for the check. My eyes blurred as I lowered them to see the amount of money printed on the line. I wiped my eyes and finally saw the cash amount for my work for *With Freckles on Her Skin* was five hundred dollars! My knees went weak. I felt close to passing out.

"This is the amount left after our fee and commission," said Miss Kayte, still smiling like the villainous Cheshire Cat in *Alice in Wonderland*. "There will be more cash flowing in for quite some time." And like Cheshire Cat, she disappeared down the hallway with Gilles at her side.

Still shaking with disbelief, I looked up from the check and saw Twiggy, my true love, hurrying toward me.

"Hi, darling! I love you, Twiggy, with all my heart." I placed my hands on her cheeks and kissed her tenderly.

"I love you, too, with all my heart," Twiggy said. "We wanted to be with you on this special day."

"Who's we?"

"Nyah!" Granny called out, waving a hand high above her head. "We see you're playing to a packed house."

"We're very proud of you, you," Claudia said, hugging me.

"We're all very proud of you, my love," Twiggy chimed. "I saw Kayte hand you a check."

I handed the check to Twiggy.

"Five hundred dollars! Honey, you have painted a masterpiece, and at such a young age. I couldn't be prouder of you. You're very talented, not to mention you're the prettiest woman I have ever had the pleasure to know." While Granny and Claudia watched, Twiggy quickly kissed me.

"Nyah, did Kayte have you sign a contract yet?" Granny asked.

"No. She only handed me this check."

"Selling your portrait to a museum would be selling yourself short," Claudia said. "We—Granny and I—strongly suggest you don't sell your portrait to a museum. It would be the end of her—*With Freckles on Her Skin,* I mean. Hold out for a private buyer. Museums are for a dead artist's work."

"Museums' art is from the past, yesterday's news, Nyah," Granny added. "Your work is new and exciting. Claudia, Alvena and Roseyl just walked in. Enjoy your day you two," Granny added as they walked toward the sisters.

"Twiggy, the past is all around us."

"What do you mean?"

"Lulu is what I mean."

"What are saying? Nyah, talk to me."

"I've been thinking about time lately, about the concepts of yesterday and today and what it all means."

"You've been thinking too much. You're pale, you look like you haven't slept in a week. Lulu's been making her appearances, hasn't she? You're going to move in with me right away. I won't take no for an answer. Your fucking house is haunted by Lulu—an apparition. She's drawing you more and more into her world. Her spirit is making you sick."

36
The Tide Has Turned
Twiggy

"Do you know how embarrassing it was to get a call from the San Francisco police department?" Mum snarled. "My friend, Chief Mitchell, called personally to tell me you'd been arrested for immoral acts and public indecency. Shit, Twiggy, what is wrong with you? What an idiot."

"Jennifer and I went to a bar after my show to have a drink and talk," I said, my heart racing and my face burning shame.

"A queer bar? Are you serious?" Mum said, pounding her fist on her kitchen counter. "If you weren't a grown woman, I'd take you over my knee and lay into you!"

"Then why don't you? You've never let my age stop you from beating me," I said, my child voice trembling.

"What are you *talking* about? Yes, I disciplined you. Disciplining you was my job. I was your *mother*. I had to teach you what was right and wrong, for Christ's sake."

"And you thought pummeling me with a two-by-four was going to teach me right from wrong? Or using Dad's leather belt buckle would make me into an upstanding citizen of this little town of yours?"

"For God's sake, Twiggy, it wasn't a two-by-four. It was a little stick. And you were in junior high, not an adult."

"It was a two-by-four, Mother! How do you think I felt trying to hide the welts on my thighs and the bruises on my arms from my friends and teachers?"

Mother slapped my face.

I slapped Mother's face.

She stretched back her arm to strike me again. But I caught her hand in a tight grasp. "This will be the last time you'll ever lay hands on me, Mother. The tide has turned."

"What do you mean, the tide has turned?"

I twisted her wrist until her knees touched the floor.

"You're hurting me! Stop it!"

"You're intelligent, Mother, so figure it out for yourself." She wrenched her hand from mine. I grabbed her arm again.

"What do you think you're doing with that artist, what's her name? She's a low-life queer. She lived at the rundown Delmonico for years. What do you see in her? Christ, she's made up a big story about finding a little girl sitting in the park in the middle of winter. Are you stupid? She's a lunatic."

"A lunatic? What about the ragdoll she found? And what about knowing exactly what the orphanage looked like before it burned to the ground?"

"She probably bought the doll at a secondhand store, and probably spent hours in our library researching her fantastic story. Jesus, Twiggy, you've always been a sucker for the down and out. Your little girlfriend lives in two worlds, the real one and her crazy one. Let go of my arm or I'll—"

"You'll what Mother?" I snapped. "Lock me in the pantry? Your dirty little secret? I'm done with you."

"Fuck you, Twiggy. Let go of me! What do you think you're doing?"

I let go of her arm; she ran toward me with the intent to shove me. I stepped aside and tripped her. When she rose again, I grabbed her and pinioned her arm behind her back. She struggled but got a grasp around my waist. We were locked in a strong body grip. Our hipbones were braced against each other. We were locked in an immovable embrace, swaying this way and that. She grunted. I stepped one foot between her feet; I had her in a deadlock. Every muscle in my body strained to hold ground, we were like two boa constrictors. But I was the stronger, and inch by inch I bent her over backwards. At last, I had her on the floor; I straddled her. With my fingers around her throat, I was unwilling to relent.

Rapidly running out of steam, I released my grip. My reflexes were slowing. She scrabbled away and stood on wobbling legs and slapped my face—slapped it hard. My cheek was on fire. The elasticity was gone from my arms. The bitch tried a sweeping right hook to my jaw but missed.

"The McGowens' brother raped Nyah's mother," Mum shouted.

"What did you say?" I shouted back, my hand in the air, ready to strike.

"Ask Granny and Claudia if you don't believe me."

I grabbed her wrist, dragged her to the pantry and shoved her inside. With the skeleton key still in the keyhole, I twisted it hard, hard enough to hear the steel lock clang into place.

"Let me out of here!" she yelled, pounding on the door.

I flipped the light switch on; for effect, I flipped the switch off. "Lights out."

I passed her husband who was pulling up in the driveway.

Drunk.

37
Hidden Secrets
Nyah

It was late summer into autumn and nothing but cobalt blue sky. An intimate warm breeze rustled the apple-red, saffron-orange, and lemon-yellow leaves of the weeping willows, as well as the leaves of the white birch forest. Scarlet-chested robins hopped here and there in the viridian-green grass feeling for the movement of ground worms under their claws. Seagulls scratched in the sand for clams, and with a wingspan of six feet, a convocation of white-headed eagles glided over the white caps of the sea, steady and ready to latch onto a pink Chinook salmon.

I'd been living in my attic since I bought Chimacum House. For hours at a time, I'd stand between the willows gazing thirteen miles out to sea, out to the end of the world. Even though I was no longer a starving artist, I continued to think like one as if a shadow were stalking me from the innermost crypts of my soul.

From behind the door of my unfinished attic space, I heard a buzzing hum of a swarm of honeybees. I opened the door. A strong scent of raw honey filled my senses. There in the dark space, several dozen cells of honeycomb clung to the two-by-four ceiling rafters. From one beam, a spider web was attached to a windowsill. Hundreds of buzzing honeybees circled around the cells and dozens entered the room through the slightly ajar window, landing on the windowsill as they entered and exited the chamber. The floor was thick with honey.

Dozens of bees flitted and buzzed around my head. I gently brushed one bee off my arm. As I was backing out of the hive, my leg bumped into something sharp. The corners of two canvas oil paintings were wedged between the wall and a large bookshelf. I slid the paintings from the hiding place and held the first up to view. The painting was a portrait of me!

My heart pounded against my ribs. My knees wobbled. I sank onto the stool. The other painting was a portrait of me as a very young girl, sitting next to the apparition I had grown to love and to fear, the little girl named Lulu. The two of us were on a turquoise Indian blanket between the weeping willow trees on Thunder Edge facing the sea with a picnic basket between us. The paintings were dated 1930. At the bottom right-hand side of the portraits were painted these words:

I ebb and flow,
I go and go.
I'll follow you,
wait for me when I do.
My Years are long,
you are where I belong. Lulu

I needed air. I ran down two flights of stairs and to the end of the embankment where my eyes were drawn to the broken-down children's graveyard. Slowly, I traipsed through the overgrown grass. A brown and black garter snake with a white stripe down its back slithered in front of me and disappeared. I jumped backward. A spider's web brushed across my brow. The hackles on the back of my neck rose. I tripped on a broken stone. I used the Lord's name in an irreverent manner. I saw it—a faded, tattered ragdoll, leaning on one of the decayed tombstones. I knelt on both knees and moved in closer. Although the stone was cracked and broken in several places, I could piece together the letters and the dates on the inscription:

Lulu McDuffy
Orphan
1883 – 1889

My nerves unraveled.

I turned around, facing my back porch. Mable and Parker were perched on the railing. Parker, the larger of the two, stood on one talon and cocked its head toward me, while manically jumping up and down. Mable flew over the willow trees, landed on a low-hanging branch, and hung upside down by her talons, bobbing her head to keep the branch bouncing. Then, clear as a bell, I heard Mable speak: *"I have to get back to you."*

The wise, yellow-eyed, great horned owl sat at the end of the railing, unblinking.

38
The Magical Season of Autumn
Nyah

Late August—the season of magic—revealed the natural process of dying and rebirth. An unusual sultry breeze blew in from the west rustling the dried leaves. The weather cock squeaked and circled counterclockwise in tandem with the spirts of the gusts. A bald eagle screeched and squawked as it glided past the drop-off point of Thunder Edge, then nose-dived toward the sea. With its spiked talons it clasped a rainbow salmon out of the crest of a wave, then, catching a ride off an upward gust of wind, it soared high toward a silver-lined cloud. A ray of sunshine pierced through the cloud and reflected off the tips of the eagle's white tail feathers. A fledgling appeared, and with wings flapping fast, it flew under the adult bird. In midair, the youngster gashed open the belly of the fish with its pointed hooked beak, releasing a slurry of guts into the hungry throat of the offspring. The long entrails dangled over both sides of its beak and set the hair on my forearms a-bristling.

During the first weekend of the summer season, a private art collector, Nanny Tarpee of Laguna Beach, bought my *Freckles* collection. Lulu had promised to make me rich, and the *Freckles* collection allowed me a comfortable life. I was an up-and-coming artist with cold hard cash in the bank, and a few coins clinking together in my pants pocket.

When summer was entering August, I'd accepted Twiggy's request to move in with her. Along with Dave's help, we were packing my belongings into several Olympia beer boxes and moving my stuff from Chimacum House into Twiggy's beach house. While Twiggy and Dave were arranging my boxes into my Starlight and Twiggy's Bullet-Nose, I scurried upstairs to my studio.

From behind the door of my unfinished attic, I heard the familiar buzzing hum of the bees. I walked to the door and opened it. The room smelled sweet, like lavender honey. Hundreds of bees circled the honeycomb cells, and the floor was sticky.

I'd left Lulu's ragdoll sitting in the corner under my easel. The honeybees ignored my trespass. The oil paintings of Lulu and me were safely secured, still wedged between the wall and the bookshelf. I grabbed the doll and sat it up in the corner of the desk. Taking in one last view of the room, I said my goodbyes, walked out the door and locked it behind me.

When I came downstairs, Dave was driving his car down the driveway and Twiggy had just returned to the living room.

"What were you doing upstairs?" Twiggy asked.

"Just saying my goodbyes."

Twiggy's third floor attic faced Discovery Bay. It had four large bay windows, two facing west into the sunset over the Olympic mountains, and the other two facing east into the sunrise over Discovery Bay. After we unpacked my beer boxes and arranged my new art studio, Twiggy went grocery shopping downtown, while I, with my Indian blanket secured under my arm, rested against one of the birch trees in Twiggy's back forty. Under the cerulean sky, with a high view of the sea, I closed my eyes. But my attempted nap was interrupted when my ears popped.

"Lulu?" I opened my eyes.

"I brought a picnic basket, fried chicken and bread," Lulu said, showcasing a grin. "Let's eat."

Lulu was wearing faded blue jeans, a cowl neck wool sweater, and red leather knee-high cowgirl boots that matched the strawberry color of her short, butchy hairstyle.

She sat on the grass, her back against my knees. We chomped on chicken legs.

"This could be ours for as long as I want it to be, forever even, or even until tomorrow." Lulu used a paper napkin to wipe her painted lips.

"Yes, but I have my life in this world with Twiggy. We're making plans for our future together."

"Twiggy isn't for you. You and I, we belong together."

"I do care about you, Lulu," I said softly, "but I'm drawn to the dream, the illusion of you."

Lulu whispered, "This day will never happen again, Nyah."

"What do you mean?"

"I'm leaving. It's time."

Faintly, the birch leaves shivered, dancing along in the gentle breeze. Lulu was gone. In her stead, leaning against my knees, was the red-cheeked ragdoll with bright red yarn hair, a triangular nose, and red and white stockings.

I grasped the ragdoll by the hand and stood resting my shoulder against the birch as the whitecaps crashed onto the shore. I heard the squeak of the rusting weathercock and felt the warm sun on my shoulders and face. I tasted the salt of the sea on my lips. I saw a large sailboat sailing westward to the open sea.

Tick tock, tick tock.

39
It Was One of Those Magical Days
Nyah

Late summer was moving into autumn, one of those mystical days that can make one's soul feel frisky, and the spell of romance was in the air. It was one of those days when a woman can fall under the spell of Aphrodite, the Greek goddess of love and passion and making a fool out of the beloved. It was one of those days that Sappho—the Greek lesbian poet of the isle of Lesbo—begged Aphrodite to help her win the love of her beloved, to ease her crushed spirit.

My corvid family, Mable and Parker, were frolicking with their family members who had flown in from as far away as Port Hadlock. They were jumping from branch to branch, hanging by their talons, swaying forward and back again, over and over—cawing loudly and enjoying the day. A hefty wind assaulted the cliff wall and produced a powerful late afternoon updraft.

And the owl was perched on the rail.

Twiggy was taking a well-deserved catnap in the hammock suspended between two of our birch trees. The tide had turned on its way inland, and I was lying on my Indian blanket in the middle of our dense meadow of scarlet and saffron poppies when I dropped into a dream.

I stood between the weeping willow trees. The leaves were in the beginning stages of autumn coloration. I stared down a craggy beach at the mountainous large boulders peppered across the sandy seashore. The early seasonal wind gusted, blowing rain at my face and down my neck. At that moment I faced myself—for the first time in my life. Reality hit me like a stone. I understood how strong nature was, how harsh she could be. Something unnatural about the way the wind smelled, how it felt on my face, how my skin popped up goosebumps. I sensed darkness itself was coming, a force not belonging on this earth. My heart raced, my pulse pounded through my neck arteries, and my skin was cold.

In spite of the warnings, I continued down the wet slope, down to the angry sea. I had little strength and could hardly stabilize my legs and footing. The wind was gaining power. Halfway down the slope, a branch from a hickory tree snapped and blew upward to where I struggled. I took one step heading back up the path, but the wind sucked the oxygen out of my lungs. I was high above the water when I saw the wave rumble onto the beach, up over the boulders, washing away the path behind me. Two squawking crows flew in a circle above my head. And I saw her.

My ears popped.

Lulu was below me trying to crawl up the slope from the seashore. Her fingers dug deep into the muddy sod. She struggled to grasp a branch along the bank. I scrambled and slipped down the embankment. I reached out for her; her hand reached for mine. In horror I stared as she lost her balance and fell backward. She slipped farther toward the seashore. Another monster wave foamed at the mouth with its maw wide open. I saw it coming—a runaway train.

I had no idea where my inner courage came from, but I skidded down the sludge against the wind. The path was wet, heavy clay. I slipped far enough through the mire to wrap my arms around Lulu's waist. I held her up out of the way of the crashing wave. The crest missed swallowing us by mere inches.

Lulu lay back against me, white, spent. Her eyes closed. Her eyelashes flickered in the wind. I thought she'd died in my arms, but her lips parted.

She said, "I was afraid I wouldn't get to you in time, Nyah, darling."

I held her close to my heaving breast. Even with those wrathful waves below us I thought I'd be able to lift her to safety. I pressed my cheek against her cheek. Her face was deathly cold. She lifted her hands slowly, heavily, as if lifting a great weight, and draped her arms around my neck.

"I had to get back to you."

"We have to hurry," I stammered. "These waves will snag another bite out of us."

I pulled and stretched my arms to their limit, dug my boots into the oozing clay, but she was dead weight. She had no strength left. She lifted her face to mine, smiling at me piteously, and shook her head.

"You go, Nyah. I can't make it."

I tried to lift her, but she was too heavy. I couldn't find a foothold on the slick slush. The sea was higher, almost at our feet. A dark ripple washed in over my ankles. "Lulu," I cried, "for God's sake."

"Let me look at you," she whispered.

I could barely hear her. She held my face in her hands and looked at me for a moment with wide, black eyes. "It's been a long time, darling."

I didn't want to talk. I wanted to get out of there. I wanted to get her up the slope away from the riptide.

"Look, if I could lift you up on my back . . ." But she didn't hear me.

"Yes," she said, mumbling as if to herself. "I was not wrong. I knew you still loved me."

"Lulu," I cried. "Please . . ."

Her arms tightened around me for a moment. "Hold me close, Nyah. We're together now."

I held her close, but my mind was in full crimson panic. I couldn't lift her; I couldn't get her loose. The ground was giving way.

"Nyah, don't fear being alone anymore. You're dreaming now. And you'll wake up and I'll be gone, this time forever. There is no magic. Nothing lives forever—except love."

"Lulu, the sea is taking you," I cried.

"Let's pretend I'll once again be with you. Let's pretend I'll sit for you, and you'll paint another portrait of me. This time I'll be standing on the deck of a wonderful big sailboat with the wind blowing my red locks and one curl covering one eye."

"Yes, let's pretend we'll see each other again. Twiggy!" I shouted as loudly as I could. "Twiggy, help me!"

I saw it coming—a vast mud-brown curl, sweeping back up toward the sea. There was no escape. We could never have climbed above it. It came in steady and wild with a strange sucking noise. *Oh, dear God, we'll go together.*

Bending over I kissed her full on the lips. "Yes, Lulu," I answered, "we're together now."

She knew the giant deluge was hanging over our heads. "Nyah," she whispered, pressing against my cheek, "there is only one love, and nothing can change our love. It's all right, my darling. Whatever happens, we'll always be together, somewhere in time."

"I know."

I tried to hold her, to go out with her, but the sea ripped us apart and the wave sucked me under. The surge of the wild torrent rolled me over and over. I felt myself flung backward, swallowed, and tossed upward again. I was choking. The wave hit me again.

"Nyah! Wake up!"

I thought I heard Twiggy's voice—muffled. But I was slipping into the sea. Cold water pounded me down. Waves sucked at me, drowning me.

"Nyah, wake up! Wake up!"

I reached toward the voice—Twiggy's voice.

"Wake up, Nyah! You're having a dream!"

Again, Twiggy's voice. I reached toward her voice. Our fingertips touched, but Twiggy slipped in the mud onto her back. She dug her heels deeper and deeper into the slush as she reached out for my hand until our hands were tightly grasped.

"Nyah, come back . . . come back to me . . ." Twiggy's voice was sounding much closer.

After I was safe at the top of the slope, I faced the sea. I saw a red-cheeked ragdoll with bright red yarn hair, a triangular red nose, and red and white stockings slowly sink into the sea.

"Nyah, wake up. You're okay now. You're safe."

I woke up in front of the hot fireplace wrapped in my Indian blanket with my head resting on Twiggy's lap.

40

A Skinny Old Woman Alone in A Closet
Nyah

Saturday evening Twiggy drew a hot bath and filled it to the brim.

"How're you feeling?" Twiggy asked me. "You're flushed and I can all but hear your heart pounding." She pressed her fingertips to my wrist. "And your heartbeat is way up, about one-twenty."

Twiggy grasped my wrist. "There you go, your heart is slowing down. Just keep breathing slowly in and out."

She guided me up the stairs and helped me sit in the pink chair in her walk-in closet and suggested I get undressed and into the tub while the water was still warm.

"I'll be downstairs if you need me," she said.

My head surely weighed fifty pounds. Bad dreams made me feel ill. I shut my eyes and rested on the back of the chair. My breath was shallow, and it was difficult to breathe. Stark naked, I noticed a quick movement in the beveled mirror on the back of the closet door. I turned and saw an emaciated skinny woman sitting in a chair and realized the skinny woman was me! I'm the skinny old woman sitting alone locked inside a closet. I pondered how quickly time ticks away: *tick, tock, tick, tock . . .*

I poked my head through the crack in the door. Twiggy was nowhere to be seen. Rose-scented steam wafting from the six-foot eagle claw tub gave me little to no pleasure. Twiggy had draped a thick bath towel over the chrome towel racks and placed a small spray bottle filled with cool rose water on the edge of the tub. I sank both feet in the inviting hot spa and slipped under the water up to my neck. I took in a deep gulp of the rose-scented mist floating above my belly. I closed my eyes. I slowly let my knees separate. My back arched as the hot water rushed inside of me and took my breath away. I heard the bathroom door quietly shut.

After soaking I pulled myself out of the tub, stepped onto the bathmat and wrapped myself in the towel. I pulled the plug and sat on the toilet seat and unwrapped the towel from my damp warm body. I put on my terry cloth robe and quietly opened the door into our bedroom. Twiggy was in bed with her arms behind her head wearing nothing but a smile. She lifted the covers inviting me into her bed.

"Come to bed, honey. I want to snuggle with you."

"I need to be alone tonight, Twiggy."

"Alone? Nyah, you're afraid to be alone. And you're afraid to be with anyone. You're stuck in emotional desperation, and you don't know how to trust your instincts."

The room lit up for a split second and a moment later, the rumbling thunder of autumn echoed over the Strait. I walked to the window.

"What are you doing over there? It's just thunder. Come over here. Lie down next to me."

"It's actually hailing. I'm tired of the weather."

"You're tired of skulking around in your private prison, Nyah. You've locked yourself up in a cocoon of madness. The prison resides inside of you and it's stifling your spirit."

A small cuckoo clock in the corner of the bedroom peeped. The little yellow bird popped out the door: *cuckoo, cuckoo.*

Twiggy said, "Time can be our companion reminding us to look ahead, to have faith, to live life fully, to leave a positive mark on the world. As a stalker, time hides in the shadow. We live our lives with our heads turned around backwards and get lost living in the past. Nyah, you have a death wish."

"I want to be alone. I have to think. I don't have a wish to die."

"You may love living, but you don't like life. You're afraid of the world. You absorb your rage into your soul. You isolate. You hide out from the world. You're basically a recluse. And most recently, you opened yourself to another world, the world where Lulu resides."

"Does your family think I'm nuts? Do you think I have a screw missing?"

"You need more rest," Twiggy said. "Don't worry about anything right now. Get some sleep. I'll be right here on the couch. I'll read."

She kissed me on the corner of my mouth. Then she said, "Something happened in San Francisco. We'll talk about it when you're rested."

"What happened in San Francisco?"

"I'll tell you later. Right now, I want you to rest."

41
Life Draining into A Crack in Concrete
Nyah

"What happened in San Francisco?"

"Okay, but don't worry. I'm all right," Twiggy said. "After my San Francisco show, an old friend and I went to a gay bar called the Black Cat Café for a drink. While we were there, the place was raided."

"Raided? For what? Were you arrested?"

"The bar's patrons are lesbians and gay men. It's a drag queen bar. Someone called the cops, and they stormed the place in full force. A riot broke out. Beer cans were thrown at the police, chairs hurled across the room, fist fights—it was a bloody mess. My friend and I headed for the back door, but there were paddy wagons in the alley with cops shoving everyone in the back.

"Even though we didn't resist, the cops were on a rampage. A couple cops raised their clubs against my friend, and she was beaten. Nyah, I was so scared. I was horrified. Jennifer was lying in the alley with her blood running into the cement. When I tried to help, another cop grabbed me in a chokehold. I couldn't breathe. I blacked out. He tossed me in the van."

"Who's Jennifer?" I asked.

"I woke up in the hospital."

"Who's Jennifer, Twiggy? Wait. You ended up in the hospital?"

"Yes, but I'm okay. Jennifer and I lived together when we were in our twenties. We loved each other. But she couldn't adapt to the prejudice and the violence against women—against lesbians. We were friends for years. Nothing else. Best friends. Now get some rest. Everything's going to be okay."

"What happened to Jennifer?"

"She didn't make it, Nyah. She was killed. And now I feel as though I'm losing you." Twiggy put her palms over her eyes. She wept as if she were seeing Jennifer bleed out, her life draining into a crack in concrete.

42
The Big Bad Wolf and the Riding Hoods
Nyah

At dusk, the cold autumn rain ricocheted off the windshield of my Starlight. I sped up the hill to Highway 20, a black and windy unlit country road. Gripping the leather-wrapped steering wheel as I came dangerously close to seventy-five miles per hour, my sweating palms stuck to the steering wheel turning my knuckles white. Faint thunder rumbled throughout the surrounding woods. I dropped the automatic transmission into second gear. The muffler growled. With the sudden drop in gear the tachometer jumped from 45,000 rpm to 65,000 rpm. My Starlight maneuvered tightly around the first of the hairpin curves and skidded, narrowly missing a fallen branch of a decayed red cedar. Cold-to-the-bone fingers clutched my throat.

"Nyah, slow down," Twiggy ordered. "We have time. Slow down."

Fifteen minutes later I pulled onto a muddy overgrown grassy sideroad, a mile past Airport Road. My headlights lit up a decaying sign nailed to a tree: NO TRESPASSING: VIOLATORS WILL BE SHOT. Thirty feet further, the road ended. I peeled my fingers off the steering wheel and slid the gearshift into park and engaged the emergency brake.

"It's now or never," Twiggy said, her voice quivering.

"So, you're sure he's allergic to bee venom?"

"Granny told me he was attacked by a swarm of bees as a kid and in a coma for several days, almost died. Granny and the McGowen sisters have been neighborhood friends since they were in their teens, and they all hated him."

We stared into the dimly lit wooded area ahead of the car. The rain pellets continued to assault the roof. I switched off the windshield wipers, and rain turned the window into a rolling opaque river, blurring the forest.

"Let's do this," I said, in a strong, even tone. I swallowed hard. Acid bile burned its way down my throat. My knees rattled.

"Grab the flashlights."

"Got 'em."

We opened the car doors and stepped onto overgrown weeds. We pushed the doors carefully shut, although no one would be able to hear our trespass a mile from nowhere. We were garbed in caps, red raincoats, and black leather boots. Instantly, the deafening pellets of rain pounded on our rain caps like BB's hurled from the heavens. Blackberry thorns as thick as human fingers—stalkers—stood in wait for unaware victims, swaying back and forth. Snake-like devil's club spines pushed upward, gnarly fingers latching around fir trees like dead Christmas lights. Blackened moss encroached upon the gravel. Twiggy stumbled into a small hole next to a rotted stump. A devil's claw tore the lower sleeve of her raincoat.

As we approached the end of the path, an old shack appeared, decrepit, gray, and surrounded by overgrown stinging nettles. The back door screen was rusted in the open position, like the forbidden mouth of a long-deserted cave. The remaining window shutters dangled by one corner while shutters that had lost the battle lay on the ground, all but swallowed by the blackberry vines. Thick branches of morning glory wove in and out of sharp jagged windows, like worms in the eyes of a dead man. The windows were boarded up with rotted planks. Narrow overgrown paths led us around to a front door facing west toward the sea.

"I've been here before, on this path," I murmured to Twiggy. "There's a dirt floor, dandelions growing out of the corners of the room. A cruddy tub and toilet, like in my nightmare. I remember two women running down this path toward the road. One was carrying me. She tripped, and I was thrown into prickly vines."

Suddenly, an owl flew over our heads from one tree branch to another, screeching, a mythical omen of evil and death.

"Fuck, I can't take this," Twiggy said.

"We have to keep going."

Snake grass, stinging nettles and thorns had choked the life out of the tall deciduous trees of years gone by. We rounded the corner to the front door. Wild ferns covered the railing. The windows on either side of the door had cracks held together with tattered gray duct tape. Heavy blankets blocked out the world. The porch listed to the left, held up with a post. A rotted, wooden rocking chair was missing three back rungs and one armrest. Next to the chair was a small table with a cracked, yellowed ash tray piled with cigarette butts—Camel straights. Some of the butts had fallen into a disintegrated crack in the porch plank. The porch had several boards missing. The steps were loose and cracked.

The collapsing shack was set back in the woods not visible from the nearby beach. We heard the rush of the tidal waters and the waves crashing the shore. Leaning against the rain-stained woodshed was a wooden ladder. I remembered the ladder like in my nightmare.

"I hear bees," Twiggy said.

"Yeah, it sounds like they're inside the rotting tree trunks under the gutter." I turned to face the house. "McGowen, come outside," I yelled, over the loud pressing rainstorm. "Your sisters sent us."

"McGowen," Twiggy hollered. "Roseyl and Alvena told us where you live. Come outside."

"McGowen!" I shouted, my heart thumping hard.

"What ya want?" he yelled, over the pounding rain. "Whoz you? Git the hell off ma property!"

"Roseyl and Alvena sent us."

"Roseyl? Alvena?"

"Yeah. Roseyl and Alvena," Twiggy shouted. "Come outside."

He switched on the outdoor light. The light blinked off and on like a strobe. We heard the chain lock being lifted. The door slowly creaked open. A blotchy, gray-bearded face peeked out the door. His bright red nose and broken blue veins spread across his face like spider webs. A filthy brown farmer's hat with a sweat-stained rim drooped over his forehead.

"Whoz you? What ya want? Git off ma property!"

"Can we talk?" Twiggy asked.

The old man opened the door and stepped onto the broken-down steps, staggered over to his rocking chair, and plopped heavily in the seat. He leaned his crooked wooden cane up against the house. He was drunk.

"I can smell your sour stench," I shouted over the pounding storm. "Can you hear me old man?"

"Whoz dat?" The old man squinted from under his hat.

"Me, old man, I'm talking to you. Don't you remember me?" I shouted.

Never taking my eyes off him, I reached inside the pocket of my raincoat, making sure the dozen bees were still in the corked vial. I clutched the vial in my hand.

"Remember me?" I asked. "Go back about twenty-five years. You kidnapped me from the orphanage. You molested me in your woodshed, up in the loft. Remember? Or were there too many little girls to remember them all?" We took two steps toward the old man.

He squirmed like an ensnared rat. He reached inside the front breast pocket of his reeking bib overalls and grabbed a crushed box of Camel straights. With trembling hands, he took a cigarette from the pack fumbling to put the cigarette between his purple prune lips. His mouth was empty of teeth. He felt around in his front pockets and grabbed a small red box of Diamond wooden matches. His gnarled fingers had dirt and mold under his fingernails, his hands unsteady. He dropped the first match and it fell through a rotted broken plank. He struck the second match over the broken head of a rusted flat-head nail protruding from the one arm of his rocking chair. The match flamed. He lit his cigarette and dragged deeply, held the smoke inside his lungs for several seconds and blew the toxins into the air. He coughed hard.

Green phlegm stuck on the edge of his cracked bottom lip and mingled in his beard. Dried, gray-yellow spit was woven like braids into scummy whiskers. His crippled legs, spread apart, exposed the dark yellow crotch of his urine-stained overalls. He was choking on his own spit and coughing up phlegm. He swallowed and coughed up more mucus and spit a mouthful of phlegm at us.

The old man slowly stood from the rocker, grabbed his crooked cane, wobbled to the door, and stepped inside the threshold. Before the door shut, I ran and kicked it open. The shove landed him on his butt. We stepped inside the house of horror.

Strewn about the dank room were empty bottles of Monarch vodka, some with broken necks, some lying flat with remnants of vodka puddled inside. On the table next to his sagging gray chair, a cracked Mason jar was half filled with a liquid smelling like putrid urine. Cigarette butts had burned dozens of holes on the side table and the armrests of the stuffed chair. Dark brown chicken bones with crusted strings of gray meat were covered with flies, some dead, some soon to be.

He grabbed his cane. "Git me off the God damn floor," he shouted.

"You molested me in your woodshed," I shouted, and kicked his belly. My hands were steady. "Do you remember who came to save me? Alvena and Roseyl. They knew what you were. Scumbag, we don't want you to live anymore, don't you see?"

I grasped the glass vial of honeybees in my sweating hand and popped off the cork. The cork rolled over the uneven cruddy dirt floor. Three honeybees crawled up the wall of the vial. He struggled to get off his butt. Hot blood shot through my veins. The room was spinning. I shook my head and took in a deep breath. The old man stood, then fell back down on his cruddy dirt floor.

"You kidnapped me and violated me," I shouted. "You're a dead man."

He spit a slimy wad of yellow phlegm on my boots.

I took a step closer to him, bent over his body, and placed the butt of my palm over his face.

"No, Nyah," Twiggy shouted, "don't touch him."

The old man reached for one of the half-empty vodka bottles but knocked over a Mason jar containing his urine. The dirt floor was hard, and the piss rolled down in a puddle by Twiggy's boots.

"Goddammit, you motherfucker!" Twiggy yelled.

I gagged on the stench and puked on his overalls. Again, I bent over his head and raised the butt of my palm over his face, but the strike failed. Bony fingers gripped my elbow. Adrenalin shot through my veins into every cell. I spun around on my heel, fully preparing to defend myself. But as my elbow flung around, my eyes connected with the blue topaz eyes of Miss Alvena McGowen.

"No, this isn't the way, Ladybug."

"What'd you call me?"

Alvena and Roseyl both wore red raincoats with attached red hoods, and hundreds of honeybees cloaked their shoulders, almost like jackets over their raincoats.

"This is your lucky day, old man." I stared into his black eyes, my breath fast and short. I took one step backward. My chest was a wildfire.

"No, Nyah," Miss Alvena said. "We mustn't leave telltale marks on him. You two go home. We'll take care of this. Go home."

Twiggy and I walked down the steps, careful to avoid the broken one. My gut dripped vengeance and green burning bile. My ears rang. My head felt like a dense tombstone.

By the light of our flashlights, we started up the path then heard the boards of the porch creak. The old man had stumbled out the door with his crooked cane waving in the air.

"Lawrence, let them go!" Alvena shouted, grabbing on to the back strap of his bib overalls. He pushed Alvena into the door frame.

I ran at him and slammed the heel of my hand into his chest. The blow knocked him back against the rocking chair. He raised the crooked cane high into the air and landed the stick on my shoulder. Twiggy ran toward him and pushed him. He lost his balance and fell off his steps. His sweat-stained farmer's hat flung off his head.

The hand of God saw to it that he'd land on top of the pile of rotted tree trunks under the gutter and on top of a yellowjacket hive filled with thousands of pissed-off wasps.

"Come you two, follow us. Hurry," said Alvena, shouting over the rain, tipping the rim of her red sailor's cap down over her forehead, rain rolling off onto the path.

The four of us took long strides toward the overgrown path. We stopped and looked back to the old man. Our eyes were stabbed by a bolt of lightning which parted wide open the blackened skies and split a rotted tree deep in the woods. Thunder moved the earth. Standing side by side, we watched the yellow long-legged wasps swarm the old man's head and viciously attack his neck and face. Another eye-stabbing bolt of lightning lit up the old man's face like a strobe light. We were motionless as he croaked for help. But his cries fell upon deaf ears as the skies opened wide and poured torrential rain onto our rain hats.

One foot of the old man was stuck in the hole in the middle of the rotted stumps. He lay on his other foot which was stuck up behind his butt. He couldn't stand and seemed to have lost his battle to live. He was slowly and painfully meeting his darkness. His throat swelled. He choked; his eyes bulged. His neck was bloody from his own fingernails as he gasped for air. The rain bounced off his staring eyeballs. His eye sockets formed water puddles that streamed down his temples. Pounding rain bounced off his mud-stained forehead and formed rivulets emptying into the tree stumps and slowly dripped into the yellowjacket hive, which pissed off more yellowjackets. His hand grasped a fistful of rotted wood. He was dead. A large splinter from the wood pointed to the angry skies.

"Nyah, look," Twiggy said. "There's jagged scar running down his scalp."

Darting its way down from the top of his head through his yellowed-gray hair and running down behind a blackened hole where an ear was once attached, a crusted, gray scar zigzagged down to the back of his jawbone until it disappeared under his frayed flannel collar.

"Long ago, the day our brother hurt you in the woodshed," Miss Roseyl said, "I struck him with a piece of wood."

"Yes, I remember," I said, memories rushing into my mind. "When I was small, in a woodshed . . . he was *hurting* me. I remember hearing a thud. His hat flew off his head. Someone slammed a heavy board against the wall. I remember blood running down his neck . . . a shadow wearing a red raincoat and a red sailor's cap. And I remember bees. *Hundreds* of bees were flitting around her. The lady was you, Miss Roseyl! You told me not to be afraid. You called me Ladybug."

"Yes, sister and I were present," said Alvena. "The two-by-four cracked his skull and tore off his ear. The scar branded him for life."

The old man died with his red bulb nose swelled and inflamed and deep blue tiny veins spread across his face like a spider's web. Fear was permanently stamped on the eyes of the dead man. The old man died with his eyes wide open.

"Sister, it's finished," said Alvena.

"Hail, Holy Queen, Mother of Mercy," the sisters prayed in unison, "our life, our sweetness, and our hope. To thee do we cry, poor banished children of Eve. To thee do we send up our sighs, mourning and weeping in this Valley of Tears."

"Oh, and Nyah," Roseyl said, "Lawrence was your father."

"What? What did you say?"

"He was our brother," Alvena shouted over the din of the rain. "So you're ours, too."

Roseyl said, "He was part of the Klan that stormed the bus transporting your mother and the other Irish immigrants to Seattle. During a stopover, he raped your mother."

"And he sexually abused you in that woodshed," Alvena said, pointing to the broken shed we'd just past."

Tick tock, hickory dickory dock.

43
Nuptials
Twiggy

Saturday, the second of September, early evening, and the full face of the man in the moon reflected off the waters of Discovery Bay, casting a warm ambiance on our back porch, where Nyah and I were scripting our civil commitment promises to each other.

Dave and Mary had offered the One-Eyed Dog as the venue for our forthcoming nuptials—to include an open invitation to the town to participate in their popular Hullabaloo Shindig on our special day, Sunday, the third of September at two in the afternoon. Alvena and Roseyl (Nyah's newly found biological aunts) volunteered to officiate the ceremony, and we'd asked Granny and Claudia (Nyah's soon-to-be grandparents-in-spirit) to be our special witnesses. Other invited guests included Kayte Berns (soon-to-be Nyah's shirt-tail relative), and Francis and his friend, Steve, Suzie and Roger, Kissoon Choo and her husband, and the one-eyed dog herself, Blinky.

Sunday, the third of September, was a most unusual day, billowy white clouds dancing through the sky, bright sunshine reflecting off the sailboats in the marina, Mable and Parker soaring above us, and Granny and Claudia driving us to the One-Eye Dog in their pink Cadillac DeVille Coupe—top down—all coming together in a symbiotic melody. Wearing our sunglasses and smiles, Nyah and I sat shoulder to shoulder in the back seat, holding hands, the warm breeze tossing our hair every which way. Along the drive, the pungent, smoky scent of sap dripping from the wounds of the birch trees tickled my nostrils.

"I like that you grew your hair out, Nyah, my love," I said, gently brushing her locks out of her eyes. "Have you had any more visions of Lulu?"

"Not since I moved in with you."

"Why do you think that is?"

"I think Lulu never realized she was dead—that she'd died in the fire at the orphanage, and that I'd lived. I think she was looking for the meaning of her life, just like the rest of us are. But I've come to realize that looking for the meaning of our lives is futile—it's like asking why does a tree grow? Lulu once asked me if I'd ever thought about the mystery of a world where life blooms and then rots. I think, at least for myself, that going about seeking the *experience of being alive*—to feel the rapture of being alive—that's the mystery. Lulu, I think, was seeking my help in her passage to death. But Lulu, like the rest of us, needed to tell her own story, and to understand her own story—and figure out how to cope with her own death. It's the experience of being alive—that's the mystery."

In that moment, when Nyah said she wants to experience being alive, I realized I, too, had been lost in existential questions and finding reasons for everything in my life—why this, why that? My answer was *just because.*

As we pulled up to the One-Eyed Dog, I asked Nyah, "Are you nervous?"

"My chest feels like two hummingbirds darting around my heart."

"Mine, too."

Granny parked the Caddy behind Dave's vehicle which was in front of the fire hydrant. Granny and Claudia escorted us to the entrance of the One-Eyed Dog.

I brushed a bee off my shoulder. Kayte was standing by and pulled open the heavy door as we approached. Dave's band was playing and jivin' to Glenn Miller's "In the Mood." When they noticed us, the guests pulled back and formed a path that ended at the front of the stage. Granny and Claudia, as our witnesses, escorted us to the stage, Granny's arm in mine and Claudia's arm in Nyah's.

Alvena and Roseyl were waiting and grinning from ear to ear. The band stopped playing. The musical octaves continued bouncing off the walls. Once the applauding and whistles died down, our ceremony began.

"Twiggy and Nyah," Roseyl asked, "have you come here, in the eyes of the Lord, to enter into union without coercion, freely and wholeheartedly?"

We chimed, "Yes, we have."

"Please join hands and repeat after me.

"I, Twiggy, take you, Nyah, to be my loving companion. I promise to be true to you in good times and in bad, in sickness and in health. I will love you and honor you all the days of my life."

"I, Nyah, take you, Twiggy, to be my loving companion. I promise to be true to you in good times and in bad, in sickness and in health. I will love you and honor you all the days of my life."

Roseyl closed her eyes and prayed aloud. "May the love of God be above you to overshadow you, beneath you to uphold you, before you to guide you, behind you to protect you, close beside you and within you to make you able for all things, and to reward your faithfulness with the joy and peace, which the world can neither give nor take away. Through Christ our Lord, to Whom be the glory now and ever more."

Alvena said, "Gracious God, spirit of life and love, we ask all blessings upon Twiggy and Nyah in their life together. May they be blessed with patience to see them through times of tensions or conflict. May they be blessed with kindness to enable them to nurture and care for one another in times of pain or sorrow. What God joins together, let no one put asunder. You two may exchange your rings."

We smiled at each other. "Nyah, will you take me as your loving companion?"

"Yes, I do."

I took Nyah's left hand in mine and slipped my gold band on her finger.

"Twiggy, will you take me as your loving companion?"

"Yes, I do."

Nyah took my left hand in hers and slipped her gold band on my ring finger.

"You may now kiss each other," Alvena said.

We placed our hands on each other's cheeks, looked into one another's eyes, and in front of God and our friends, we kissed.

The crowd in the One-Eyed Dog cheered and clapped.

Granny and Claudia shared the microphone. "Here they are, Twiggy and Nyah, who, from this day forward will be known as a couple with no less respect than anyone else in our town. Please enjoy the food and have fun!"

Again, our friends cheered and clapped, circling us and shaking our hands. The band swung back into gear and the dance floor once again vibrated to the foot-stomping joy of boogie-woogie dancing — the sheer joy of just being alive. We were congratulated and hugged and plied with cake and ice cream for at least an hour before we were pulled away.

"Twiggy, Nyah," Granny shouted over Glenn Miller, "Claudia and I have a surprise for you!"

"Follow us," Claudia chimed in.

With Nyah and me trailing them, they led the way to the marina across the way. We walked down the gangplank and stopped in front of Claudia's white and blue sailboat, the tell-tails flapping in the warm breeze.

"Are we going for a sail?" Nyah asked. "Whose boat's this?"

"It's Claudia's second love," I answered. "Her name is *Tick Tock*."

"Let's get on board," Claudia said, her voice cracking with emotion.

The deck held four chairs and was decorated with balloons and graffiti, a huge pink bow tied to the helm.

"She's our honeymoon gift to you two," Granny said, her voice filled with excitement.

"What do you mean?" I gasped.

"We mean, *Tick Tock* has new owners—you and Nyah," Granny said, proudly standing with both hands on her hips.

"She's a twenty-five-foot, 1942 single-mast, clinker-built, Nordic Folk boat," Claudia said with pride.

Smiling at me, Granny said, "We've been teaching you the craft of sailing since you were in the third grade. And now's the time to pass on our legacy. And Kissoon has your luggage packed and ready." Granny's grin was as wide as the Cheshire cat's.

"Packed and ready for what?" I asked.

"You want to tell them?" Claudia asked Granny.

"Nah, you go ahead."

"The four of us, Granny, myself, and you two, we're sailing to Doe Bay."

"What?" Nyah blurted. "We're going *sailing?* But I can't swim!"

Still grinning, Granny announced, "You're in good hands, Nyah. Claudia was the first woman to win the Scotland swimming championship back in 'ninety-two, at the mere age of twenty-five. And besides, there's six lifesaver rings onboard."

"Claudia," I said in wonder, "I didn't know that you were a champion swimmer. You never shared that with me."

"I'm not one to toot my own horn."

"Yes, you are," Granny teased.

Tearing up, I said, "Claudia, I don't know what to say."

Granny put an arm around both of us. "Consider the *Tick Tock* our way of saying thank you."

"Thanking us for what?" I asked.

"For reminding us of what's important. Twenty-four-hours of solitary confinement didn't teach my daughter anything. To quote *Alice's Adventures in Wonderland,* your mother was as mad as the Mad Hatter when you locked her in her own pantry."

"Her husband called us and told us what happened," Claudia said. "Apparently, when he woke from his stupor, he opened the pantry and found her sitting in the corner cuddled up with a twenty-five-pound sack of flour. She hasn't spoken a word ever since."

"I'm not sorry," I said. "I feel free for the first time in my life. A huge weight has been lifted from my shoulders, and my soul is healing. I have courage that I've never had before; I'm free to live my life in a manner that suits me. And, I have Nyah's love and support."

"Twiggy, life is short," Claudia said, turning to Granny. "We have to find happiness wherever we can find it. The clock is ticking."

"Where's Doe Bay?" Nyah asked, clearly still wary about being blown off the *Tick Tock* in a squall.

"Nyah, you make me laugh," I said, taking her hand in my own. "Doe Bay's in the San Juan Islands—on the west beach of Orcas Island. It's the island Granny and Claudia and I have sailed every autumn since I was a teen."

"But, before we go," Granny said, "we have *another* surprise for you two."

"What do you mean—before we go?"

"You'll see," Granny said. "Drop down into the cabin and take a peek."

I looked at Nyah, shrugged, and opened the hatch. "After you, my dear companion." Nyah went down the steps into the cabin, and just before I stepped down, I smiled at Granny and Claudia.

Nodding knowingly, Granny said, "We'll see you two in in the morning, just before sunrise."

"Thank you both," I said fervently.

I joined Nyah below. The scent of roses filled the cabin, as well as the vision of other romantic symbols: a champagne bottle in a galvanized pan plunged deep into ice shavings, two crystal flutes next to the champagne, and draped crepe paper in all the colors of the rainbow tied to the ceiling light switches. Several red rose petals sprinkled our pillows. A note lying on the pillow read:

> *Dear Twiggy and Nyah,*
> *Once the four of us dock at Doe Bay, Claudia and I will*
> *be taking the San Juan ferry tour around the San Juan*
> *islands, then we'll pop up to Port Roberts, then taxi to*
> *Victoria, BC. We have the honeymoon suite reserved on*
> *the eighth floor of the Empress Hotel in beautiful*

downtown Victoria. Our suite has a bird's eye view overlooking the inner harbor. Claudia has always wanted to stay at the Empress and tour beautiful downtown Victoria, and so have I. We're bringing our Kodak Brownie and plan on taking dozens of photos at the Butchart Gardens.

Twiggy, you are an excellent sailor and we trust you two will have a wonderful honeymoon. We love you. Granny and Claudia.

Nyah took the note from my fingers and as it fell to the floor, she unbuttoned my jeans, pulled them past my hips, and let them fall on the pink carpet. I pushed off my tennis shoes with my toes and shook off my jeans. Nyah pulled my sweater up above my arms. She kissed my neck and suckled my breast while my hands were above my head, then helped me lie down.

Nyah whispered, "It's the experience of being alive—that's the mystery."

44
Sailing Into the Sunrise
Nyah

"Permission to board!"

"Twiggy, wake up," I said. "Granny and Claudia are here."

I stepped up the ladder, threw back the hatch, and emerged into the dawn. "Permission granted," I told them.

"We brought breakfast," Claudia said, giving me a bearhug. "Leftovers from the party."

"Where's Twiggy?" Granny asked, just as Twiggy popped her head up from the hatch.

"Good morning!" Twiggy said, her sleepy voice crackling. "Granny, is that a thermos of hot coffee, I hope?"

"It is."

Claudia said, "Shall we have a bit of breakfast in the cabin?"

Granny and Claudia followed Twiggy as she stepped back down the stairs, and I trailed behind. While Granny poured coffee, and Claudia set out plates on the table, I straightened the blankets on our honeymoon bunk, smiling ear to ear, recalling the best lovemaking of our relationship.

"Smile," Claudia said as she pressed the button on the Kodak Brownie camera. "Gran, give them the cash."

"Cash?" Twiggy said. "What cash?"

Claudia said, "We stopped in at the One-Eyed Dog before we got here, and Dave and Mary handed us this envelope with over a hundred bucks in it. The guests donated to your trip. And this other envelope is loaded with cash, too, from Gran and me. Everyone wishes you both all the love in the world."

"Really?" Twiggy said. "I could cry."

"No crying on your honeymoon," Granny said. "Let's set sail."

► ■ ◄

Just as the sun was rising in the east, Twiggy switched on the bilge pump and let it run for a minute or two. Then she turned on the running lights and set the marine radio to Channel 16—the emergency channel.

It took a good bit of navigating to get through the narrow channel. The tide and the wind—both had to be just right, and that morning the breeze was on our side. Easily, we were able to negotiate the breeze and the tide and safely set sail into the bay.

Fort Casey came into view. My heart raced, and my heart filled with love, and oh, how I loved the sea!

The wind snapped the sails. The green water rushed by, slapping against the sides of the hull. Sailing was a creation unto itself, a crystalized sea of never-ending blue life, steady winds, sometimes a slight breeze, sometimes a howling menace.

Mable and Parker were hanging upside down on the top rigging like clothes on a laundry line drying under the sun. They spread their wings and launched into the air, catching a ride on an updraft. Soaring high into the wind, they dove, landed on a foot-long piece of driftwood, and surfed behind the wake of the boat. Slipping this way, then that way, they dug all eight of their claws into the bark and maneuvered it perpendicular to their bodies. Suddenly, they stopped frolicking. They spread their wings, and a breeze lifted them above our heads.

They landed on the port rail, facing Thunder Edge. Chimacum House was burning!

Twiggy pulled back on the throttle and turned off the engine. I rushed to the bow and dropped anchor until I felt it settle securely between rocks on the seabed.

Through the early autumn-colored leaves of the weeping willows, we watched the flames reach higher and heard the angry, passionate inferno sizzle and hiss—like a rattlesnake. The black, smoking tornado curled upward attempting to smear the face of the sun.

A moment before the roof caved in, a small red-headed girl, standing between the weeping willows, leaned forward, to the edge. With a fire-breathing dragon at her back, she fell to her Glory onto the jagged rocks on the beach below—leaving behind her longing to be of this world.

"Lulu missed out on the mystery," I said. "She was never able to experience the rapture of just being alive."

After a few moments, Twiggy said, "You once said Lulu told you she wanted to travel and to learn about history. Maybe she did travel, and maybe she learned about history as a witness to our future—reporting on events that haven't happened yet. Maybe she found a way to experience the rapture of just being alive, in her own way. Maybe that was your gift to her."

"How'd I do that?"

"You gave her an audience. Seems to me Lulu had no idea she was dead and that she was hovering between feeling obsolete and dead. You may have helped her feel relevant. And your wish was to be well-known in the art world. Lulu made you famous. Maybe that was Lulu's gift to you."

"Thanks, Twiggy. That's what I'll remember—the gifts of love people share with each other." I turned my attention to our boat. "I'll weigh anchor and then we'll be off."

While I made my way to the bow, Twiggy switched on the bilge pump and let it run for a minute or two. I weighed anchor from the rocks below. Then I saw it. That damned ragdoll of Lulu's was hung up on the anchor's hook!

I reached over the rail, unsnagged the doll from the anchor, and tossed it. As the rotating whirlpool swirled counterclockwise, the doll was sucked beneath the waterline. The last I saw of it was two black button eyes staring into the abyss.

"How'd it go?" Twiggy asked, as I returned to her. "It looked like you had a fish or some other debris on the anchor."

"Just a bit of kelp. I took care of it."

Twiggy switched on the motor, and with Mable and Parker soaring high above the wind, we set sail into the timeless sunrise.

About the Author

Sandra was born and raised in the Pacific Northwest in the small settlement of Lowell, Washington, up the hill from the lush green Snohomish River Valley with an alluring view of the Cascade Mountain range. At the age of nine she penned her first two Hitchcockian mystery stories while sitting in an abandoned shack next to the railroad tracks on the banks of the raging Snohomish River. The setting for her first novel is a town nestled between the Cascade and Olympic mountains, notoriously known for its spectral figures darting about turn-of-the-century Victorian homes and buildings.

When she's not writing, Sandra enjoys painting with watercolors, working in her vegetable gardens, and experiencing fun times with her friends.

Acknowledgments

Thank you, Katherine V. Forrest, for your editing expertise and for your encouragement and patience in the earlier stages of my manuscript. Especially helpful was the education you offered me in regard to the history of violence and harsh prosecutions against lesbians in San Francisco and other Bay areas in the 1950's.

Thank you, Kay Grey, for taking on the challenge of editing my story in the later stages of my work.

And lastly, my special thanks go out to Lori L. Lake, publisher of Launch Point Press, without whose guidance in this long and arduous effort, I would still think myself a hack.

I would be amiss if I did not mention my lifelong friends, dating back to the third grade, who have always believed in me. Thank you, Beth Buckley, Cathy Campbell-Greenshields and hubby Doug, Mari Bliss-Davis, Barbara Baker-Corallo, Dr. Mary K. Gilles, Ph.D., Dr. Paula Bennett, Ph.D., and Marnie Kathryn Hargraves (1949-2020).

And thanks go out to my Gooseberry Point Book Club members to include Mary Ellen Jones (1931-2020).

Sandra Leigh Gable
Camano Island, Washington
May 2022